James Louis Hagerty is a retired highway engineer from the Maryland State Highway Administration who is a middle child of five, so enough said. For more details, see his previous book, *Just a Collection of Recollections About Stuff That Really and Truly Happened As I Recall.* (What a shameless self-promotion.)

To my mom, Elizabeth and my adopted grand mom, Patricia, the former in heaven and the latter on her way there as I write this, both colorful firebrands with the gift of gab that I took advantage of shamelessly.

To my brother and long-term housemate, Michael (Higgins), who showed that our individual pasts can be interesting and applicable to our daily lives, even if you find it chock full of many closely related scoundrels.

James Louis Hagerty

Learning How to Let It Go in the Shadow of the Belvedere

Austin Macauley Publishers™
LONDON • CAMBRIDGE • NEW YORK • SHARJAH

Copyright © James Louis Hagerty 2023

All rights reserved. No part of this publication may be reproduced, distributed, or transmitted in any form or by any means, including photocopying, recording, or other electronic or mechanical methods, without the prior written permission of the publisher, except in the case of brief quotations embodied in critical reviews and certain other non-commercial uses permitted by copyright law. For permission requests, write to the publisher.

Any person who commits any unauthorized act in relation to this publication may be liable to criminal prosecution and civil claims for damages.

This is a work of fiction. Names, characters, businesses, places, events, locales, and incidents are either the products of the author's imagination or used in a fictitious manner. Any resemblance to actual persons, living or dead, or actual events is purely coincidental.

Ordering Information
Quantity sales: Special discounts are available on quantity purchases by corporations, associations, and others. For details, contact the publisher at the address below.

Publisher's Cataloging-in-Publication data
Hagerty, James Louis
Learning How to Let it Go in the Shadow of the Belvedere

ISBN 9781649799005 (Paperback)
ISBN 9781649799012 (Hardback)
ISBN 9781649799029 (ePub e-book)

Library of Congress Control Number: 2023904584

www.austinmacauley.com/us

First Published 2023
Austin Macauley Publishers LLC
40 Wall Street,33rd Floor, Suite 3302
New York, NY 10005
USA

mail-usa@austinmacauley.com
+1 (646) 5125767

To Ms. Emma Johnson and the entire Staff at Austin Macauley Publishers who know when someone is green, but they never get mean, enabling your work to look keen and make the scene.

Table of Contents

Chapter One: The Gauntlet Has Been Thrown Down	11
Chapter Two: Beating Back Modern Day Corruption	22
Chapter Three: The Meeting	30
Chapter Four: Meeting People	46
Chapter Five: Making a Call and Calling Upon	67
Chapter Six: Out and About	75
Chapter Seven: Tying up the Loose Ends	143

Chapter One
The Gauntlet Has Been Thrown Down

The son-of-a-bitch did not recognize me at all, I was now a full head higher and had the Joe cool yuppie haircut, but I sure as hell could have picked him out of any crowd. He still looked like that overly well-groomed G.I. Joe that I had when I was a kid, the one that came along later after the first G.I. Joe with the styled beard, quaffed hair and sideburns. Even stupid kids of ten knew there was something wrong with that 8-inch-tall plastic government issued 'warrior.' Of course, the bastard may not have seen me clearly as I stood at the 3rd stall door offering more paper towels to stop the bleeding from the two teeth of his that had just been knocked down his weasel throat. Here a kid from nowhere flings open your stall door handing you paper towels and all you can think about is your sorry ass. No wonder he didn't remember me and it was a few years back after all and I had come into my own in the interim, where he had only aged and grayed.

Mr. Francis Taybeck, chief of the contracts section, would not look so pretty now had my brothers allowed me to exact some revenge on him some three years ago when I was but fifteen and the old bastard in his mid-forties. Now looking back, it was then uncharacteristic of me to be so volatile, so focused with anger, to overreact to just another serving of bull shit that happens in life, with such seething in my mid-teens. No, this was not absolutely true as I was always a hot head, to control my temper was the exception, to lose it was the rule. Had the old guy hit our mother, or cussed her, or made a move on her, then both of my brothers as well as my little sister would have all thrown down on him and ripped the old guy a new one.

This talking meticulously groomed version of the G.I. Joe went out of his way to publicly demean my mom in delivering her the bad news that came down from on high that due to her overuse of sick leave, for bouts of fatigue that caused her to sleep her lunch hour away and an extra hour here and there on the cold vinyl couch in the ladies' room, her services for the state of Maryland were no longer needed.

My brothers had seemed oblivious to mom's growing pain in the shoulders and arms that started shortly after a lifting injury at work. She was a secretary, but as was the practice of the state, her duties, like all other employees, included "all other duties as deemed necessary by your supervisor," an all-inclusive catch all, to exploit the insecure, the exploitable. Mr. Taybeck was all for equal work, equal pay. No special treatment for women and to support his philosophy, he didn't mind her lifting cartons of heavy proposal books from the floor to over her head to place on top of file cabinets on a regular basis. "What's good for the goose is good for the gander," he would self entertainingly quip when the cartons of heavy books came in every two weeks.

I very clearly remembered mom complaining about the sharp pains in her chest repeatedly, all the while watching keenly for signs of her discomfort that she tried to mask from me and the rest of our family, successful in her charade with them maybe, but not with me. One night it got so bad, she was crying, the pain she confided only to me, her middle child, was then piercing. In no time, we were in the emergency room, I being accustomed by then to the regular onslaught of the slings and arrows of life beginning even at the age of five, far more so than any joys of society's rants about the carefree happiness of youth, was more than certain it was a heart attack. It wasn't though, they didn't know what it was. A whole decade more would pass before they really started to understand about the ravages of her rheumatoid arthritis that had set in the injured area caused by the regular hefting of full boxes of thick proposal books while Mr. Taybeck watched taken some sick warped satisfaction in this, his reply to women's rights and their demands for equal treatment. Deep down, he detested females other than when his hormones caused him to briefly need them now and then. As the rheumatoid arthritis caused by the injury ravaged her body, she grew weaker and more weary, sicker as time went on. Now, owing to only her dandy of a supervisor's insistence to do so, upper management was letting her go. As luck would have it, I was home that mid-week workday, while my brothers and sister were all in school. When Mom called that day, I remembered that she wasn't crying, but just sounded so beaten down, so utterly exhausted, so wrung out, like she had already cried herself out. Being the worry wart and all-around fatalist of the family, I knew what she was about to say before she said it. I had kept track of all her sick days that she had needed over the last six months, the fact now was that she had exhausted the months of a sick leave that she was fortunate enough to accrue over her nine years before her injury in the office. My mother had always instilled in us kids that to make fun of disabled or sick people, to pretend to be sick was a sin and that you would get paid back for doing such a mean and despicable thing, in kind, meaning karma. I didn't believe people of my mother's generation knew the word karma as it only came to be after that one former Beatle who sang about it – *Instant Karma*.

She whispered into the phone, Taybeck had made a big presentation, a circus spectacle at her desk giving her the termination papers in front of her co-workers that she had been with since she started there, then he walked into his office and closed the door behind him, leaving her stunned and crying, embarrassed and ashamed for all to see. Like so many sheep, none of them came forward to comfort her. She just grabbed her purse and left, stooped shoulders from embarrassment, grabbing her chest in pain from the rheumatoid arthritis.

When I finally got there off the bus an hour later, Mom's desk was already cleared off and she was nowhere to be seen, no one else was in the large office either. That was good I guess, as I really planned to work over Mr. Taybeck as a payback. If not by fists, then with a chair or two.

I knocked on the ladies' room door and an older lady in a wheel chair pried open the door, I pulling it open all the way. It was "Miss. Tina." I had met her before when she came to our house for New Year's Eve when I was about eight, except she could walk then. Miss. Tina, usually an outspoken firebrand Italian lady was quiet and just pointed to the stair well door, all the while her eyes flitting here and there, back and forth as if she was waiting for a monster to come out of the hallway.

In the stairwell was Mom, sitting with her back to the wall side of the stairs, the wall railing side. On the other railing leaned a man, a little younger than my mother, sandy hair, a ruddy complexion that look like Paul Newman without all the gloss. He was smoking a cigarette dragging it in deeply and exhaling like he was winded from running a mile. In shape for sure, of a military gruff deport even though he was now leaning on the rail talking softly, gently to my mother, while she held her head to the side, looking blankly down the stairs. So, this was the infamous Taybeck, I had my work cut out for me no doubt. With all the strength I could muster with one arm, while still holding the stair way door with the other, I launched a sucker punch that I hope would cause him to either fall over the railing down the center of the stairwell all the way to the bottom six floors below or just knock him down a few stairs so that I being above him could then easily kick him in the ear. Mother nature's bull's eye as my street fighter older brother, Bernie had told me. Of course, none of that happened. My fist was grabbed midair and simultaneously he didn't punch my face with his other arm or twist my arm off, but instead smiled a confident smile, his blue eyes twinkling, looking now all the more like Paul Newman. There was no malice shown at all. "And what do you think you are doing, young man?" my mother said as if I had just used the wrong fork at some swanky restaurant and not just tried to kill this man in front of her. "Sending this pretty boy old creep, back to hell," I replied. For I had never seen Taybeck actually, only heard about his perpetually peacock grooming and preening for females that he secretly despised. Had I seen him before though, I would have realized this guy before me, was not of that superficial ilk, the plastic overly well-groomed G.I. Joe sort, but the genuine article all around.

The man just smiled and loosened his iron clad grip on my puny fist and pulled me to him, while shaking my hand in greeting at the same time. "Your Betty's middle boy, huh, she brags on ya' all the time."

"Go fuck yourself, Taybeck."

Mom quickly looked up from staring down the steps mindlessly, dejected and said to me, "That will be enough, you weren't raised in the gutter."

"Son, I'm not that piece off shit, Taybeck; sorry Betty, but if it's any solace to you, and you feel that you must talk to him now, he's down hall, in the men's room, 3rd stall, trying to find his two teeth that scratched my ring here."

Mr. Koehn held up his marine corp. ring with smudges of red now in the gold, and said, "Let it go." John, Mr. Koehn's first name I later found out, said he was waiting for me and he would now drive both of us home. He was one of those 'Helpers' that Mr. Rogers of TV fame had talked about on his show when I was a boy. A kind, strong, confident in knowing what was right, with compassion and respect for all who were due it, but who withheld it as needed, from those that deserved none.

Time went by, my mom rested at home and without the stress she seemed to be getting better somewhat, though still always tired. John hired me off the street when I graduated high school, and mentored me, sent to school on the State's dime and then gently nudged me out of his office to bigger things on my way in the world. Taybeck resigned very shortly from the State after his restroom dentistry session and went to work for the city. We got photos from someone showing John carrying a box of Mr. Taybeck's office and desk crap to Taybeck's car and unceremoniously dumping it all over the hood and open street aside his car. John purposely had included several of the state's heavy metal staplers, hole punches and a few of the buildings landscaping paver bricks as a goodbye gift that did not play well with the car's hood, but Taybeck never protested and just drove off with all the sheep in his old office watching it all from their sixth-floor perch.

Now the tables had turned. How many creeps work for the city are named Taybeck after all? It was him. It took all I could do to keep from throwing my hot coffee, accidentally, of course, in this sorry excuse for a human's face. I was an adult now, and it was now my turn at bat, but even though John had left the field, as it were, his confident "Let it go, Son", still lingered. This scum was pitching a million dollar plus above cost construction claim for my review and approval all the while with a shit eating grin on his face, not knowing that I was aware that the contractor involved was his buddy and even got him the city job after he had lost two teeth in that stall at state highway some five or six years ago.

I heard nothing of this clown's transmittal presentation, just a loud hollow rushing in my ears, my face must have been beat red as was the case every time I was about to lose my temper and go off. I could feel the heat in my cheeks and forehead. But in the end, I got the gist of what he was pitching to me. "Thank you, Mr. Payback, I'll call you when I'm done with my analysis to discuss my findings." The worm talked and dared to correct me. "That's Taybeck," he mumbled while smiling broadly. I swear I could then see those two new five-year-old replacement teeth, sitting side by side that were of a much brighter shade than the others in the that cheesy ass kissing smile of his and that made me smile for which I'm sure this slug mistook for friendliness. My use of "payback" while maybe consciously unintentional, was a Freudian slip I've no doubt, portending of things to come for him.

All modesty aside, I was the better man, (not saying too much considering I was the only other person then in the room) in control, confident, like John was in that stairway. But old habits die hard. As I followed the slime as it slithered out of the conference room, I grabbed hold of the wide dark blue indelible presentation marker, that I had just bought that morning from my briefcase during our meeting for just this purpose and readied it for action by pre-removing the cap, and ran the marker tip half way down this joker's back of his crème color suit jacket when I accidentally, or inadvertently sounds even better, 'bumped' into him from behind in leaving the conference room. Old habits die hard, I guess.

The contractor, who had made this claim was reputable, an old company, but of late, there were reports of substandard work, of a high turnover of the old timers in the management, of subcontractors not being paid, in short, a marked slippage in reputation. But that was not my concern. If a man earned a fair buck, then he should be paid a fair buck. Make him whole, no rewards for unforeseen issues on the job-just make them whole again, don't stick it to the contractor. Be fair and if an issue was on the fence, then let them have it, we had the deep pockets after all.

But very soon into my review, things weren't adding up. On site conditions that he claimed cost him additional money, that would have or should have been evident to anybody, were claimed to be not known by this contractor. The claim itself contained language not of a construction contractor, but that of a lawyer. 'Implied concept by owner', 'wholly unforeseen and unexpected latent condition.' Where was the good faith working relationship, we once enjoyed? The specific claimed cash outlays associated with components of the million dollar plus bamboozle were too pat as well. No item of work ever calculated out to be an odd dollar and cents amount when totaled out, but always a nice round, even one. It all appeared to have been reverse engineered from a sought-after grand total.

Be that as it may, a fair in depth review and analysis of the claim was performed and a total of fair compensation amount for extra work was arrived at which happened to be a million dollars, short of the sought-after amount which was $1,064,000. My work in the analysis was so challenging, so elaborate, that the fact that Mr. Taybeck was involved, was soon lost and forgotten and honestly had no bearing on the review.

After the report of findings was made known, all hell broke loose. It was ordered by my Powers-to-Be that a second look was to be made, which resulted in the same findings that I had determined to be correct the first time around, then at great cost the whole matter was farmed out for an outside independent review. The same findings again, go figure.

Now it was evident to everyone that something else was up, but what?

While out on our semiannual secret, yet known to all fire drill, while I was shivering in my short sleeves in the unreasonable frequent spring chill of Baltimore, next to the strip clubs on the infamous Baltimore Red Light District – 'The Block', along with the early arriving strip dancers and left over rummies from the night before (this being our pre-designated fire and bomb safe spot across the street from our office building), a Wall Street looking type 'suit' came walking right up to me and gave me this manilla envelope, bulging with papers, so much so the one corner of the envelop was ripping open. My co-workers, standing out waiting with me to go back in when the "all clear" was sounded, kidded me that it was cocaine or better yet filled with lottery scratch off tickets or ladies' pantries from old conquests. Or just a garden variety bribe being paid to yet another Maryland official.

Actually, inside were three different complete regional newspapers and a magazine with articles circled and highlighted that told of an upcoming planned acquisition of the grand old, stately Baltimore historic hotel, The

Belvedere by a local developer/contractor who planned to turn it into condos and make a killing. The contractor was the very same that had brought the claim that was a million dollars too high per two official extensive reviews and wonders of wonders the papers revealed that this particular contractor was a very close and trusted friend of the governor – actually not papers proved this, but photos. Copies of loan applications also showed that to close the deal on buying the Belvedere, a million dollars was still needed. It all made perfect sense now, the pieces all fell into place. All heretofore cool, calm and collective behavior on my part went out the window and Taybeck, the sniveling scum that presented this sham again rose in my cross hairs. It would be nice to say that my driving force here was to uncover and lay bare this whole ugly business with all its players, including all the way up to the governor himself and that this now quickly ignited red hot passion burning in my head was borne out of a deep-rooted sense of right and wrong, but it wasn't. I've always wanted to crush that bug Taybeck and the rest would just be collateral damage, providing a noble cloak of purpose to cover a very base and basic act of pure revenge for how my mother had been treated at his woman hater hands. I have my priorities after all. Getting the rest of the gang would be gravy, as it were, Although I didn't vote for that particular governor, for his second term anyway

Chapter Two
Beating Back Modern
Day Corruption

Work within an old city is especially prone to this kind of gaming the system with fraudulent claims of extra work when it comes to public works and rebuilding a very old crumbling infrastructure. In particular, one very expensive case comes to mind. When excavating for the Baltimore Underground Metro (subway for the non-hipsters) extension between from around City Hall to a few miles more up north to the venerable Johns Hopkins Hospital.

While tunneling, a few reports started coming in that people living in the vicinity of the work were now smelling gasoline fumes in their homes. We who governed the work, were suspicious. We expected a slew of claims of wall cracks when we used explosives and heavy equipment underground and were prepared to the extent of taking a costly pre-construction survey and photos of all of the private properties in the immediate vicinity of our construction work, inside and out when given permission so as to be able to later discern between existing damage caused by age and new damage caused by our operations.

Everybody wants a big payday, that proverbial 'Check' when "The man comes through with deep pockets."

Well, the construction caused damage claims never rolled in like we had expected. Baltimore folks for the most part are more honest and have more integrity than most others, a fact we, and our worldwide experienced consultant partners learned.

The claims that came in though were only of old gasoline smells in the basement of homes and businesses along our construction path. Maybe a variation on the physical damage claim scam to circumvent our pre-construction surveys we thought. How jaded and untrusting we, who held the public trust, had become. How could there be gasoline smell as all our heavy equipment used only diesel fuel? As bureaucrats often do, we pooh-poohed these claims away after a cursory, 'we really don't give a tinker's damn investigation.' Still the reports came in. People were now even falling ill. We stayed the course of plausible deniability or an engineering variation of that, that is until a few months later, when the problem literally came home to roost as they say.

When returning to the office one early afternoon after my regular lunch time walks, I finished my exercise routine with a seven floor climb up to my office. A body like mine just doesn't happen.

At first the smell was barely detectable, much like if one spilled a bottle of cleaning fluid in the stairwell, but bit by bit, day after day, the smell became overpowering and now smelled of raw gasoline. Now it was a real problem-as it affected me directly. Very soon forces were mustered, money was spent, and multiple investigations begun. My health was being jeopardized, now things just got real. While modern engineering design attempts to cover every contingency, we nor our consultants ever considered that after centuries of use and reuse, the soil of an old city can and does retain the byproducts of lives gone by. Left alone and let be, these spilled concoctions of days of old may be innocuous and benign, but when compressed air, (used to combat the 'bends' within the workers bodies as they toil in the deep tunnels being dug for the subway extension) leaked out through joints and seams in the tunnel into the nearby oil and gasoline saturated soil, (that had accumulated over the decades in areas of old fashion gas stations with single wall, leaky tanks), then the fumes from the long ago leaked gasoline and oil will migrate, be pushed along. These fumes and material were being pushed by the leaking compressed air right up to and into adjacent basements of homes. A chain is as strong as its weakest link. We paid dearly for that over sight. From then on, we placed the onus to thoroughly investigate existing site conditions on all potential contractors seeking public work and my new position of claims analyst was then also created. I guess I got the job, because I started the official bitching about the Metro, gasoline permeated soil fume migration problem. That and that I was a born Irish fighter. The position of claims analyst was newly developed in response to, well there is just no other way to say it, contractors raping and pillaging the public's transportation fund. What started as a competitive bid, lean working machine, degraded, as often happens if an industry is left to its own devices, to a snake pit of a few, prime, corrupt players who collude together to partake of a very cash enriched pie. the honest, upright players are soon edged out, or leave the field in disgust.

The sketchy contractors soon learned that they could submit unrealistically low bids, and then make their real money after award of the contract on claimed, extras and/or changed conditions that "they could not have reasonably expected", as in delays caused by unusual weather or circumstances beyond their control, or in conditions at the job site that they could not have reasonable learned of during a pre-bid investigation, such as unrecorded, underground utilities, unusual stone out crops or low load bearing soils.

In my short time reviewing such claims, they started to come in in much larger numbers, were more creative (or outlandish depending on the side of the negotiating table you sat on) and some were even getting de facto political sponsorship by friendly politicians.

I though, was the right person for the job as I was never motivated by money, I was a civil servant after all. Not by prestige either, as the field of engineering is seldomly in the public's eye, and never by politics as that red flag waving before me makes me see red, through and through. Like it or not, the cross I have to bear, is that I am motivated more by paybacks, revenge, enmity and vindictiveness. I like to fight. I like the contest. So the quagmire, the filthy swamp I had stumbled into suited me just fine.

They cursed me, tried to go around me, tried to get me fired. I just kept smiling, killing them with kindness and following the paper trails. After a while you get a reputation of fighting and good people come to you with the goods. Anonymous phone calls, where to look, notes dropped on your desk, bulging stuffed manilla envelopes anonymously handed to you while you are freezing outside a titty bar waiting for your office's fire drill to be over. It was rewarding work.

Once, while in negotiation over a particularly, fat, juicy, but totally fraudulent, meritless claim for additional cost, my second, (you always have at least two members of a negotiating team so as to verify or deny later claims of promises that often materialized post settlement) had to leave the room. As soon as the latch on the door clicked close, the contractor slid a bulging, open envelope toward me. I could see hundred-dollar bills. Evidentially, this guy didn't get the memo about me. For a nano second, I mused about Southern France, under an assumed identity, but then strains from the movie *Deliverance* with the dueling banjos popped in my mind and I just pushed the envelope back and calmly said, "I am too pretty to go to jail. Don't you think?" He took back his envelope.

The claim that started this tale was one of those unbelievable, meritless, laughable, bold face fraudulent but politically connected ones. A classic one that piqued my interest. The work itself wasn't world shaking…not a tunnel, nor a bridge, not even new construction, but a relatively minor bridge superstructure and bridge deck rehabilitation. As was almost always the case, the contractor discovered a unique facet of the work site that could be grossly exploited once he was awarded the contract, in this case it didn't actually involve the structure itself, but the soil far below the structure. While the contractor's work was all on the structure itself, we required demotion debris shields over the side to protect the environment. Simple enough, we even provided conceptual drawings giving an example of how the shields could be temporarily supported from the structures steel superstructure elements-the outside edge stringers, then comes the fly in the ointment, as it were. The contractor would rather support the debris shields from the soil surface far below using elaborate steel tower bent structures. We thought it very odd, quite expensive and not necessary, but it was his call as long as he fulfilled the requirement of supplying the debris shields. We said yes and approved.

Then, surprises of all surprises, the contractor said that his elaborate costly, support system from the soil below up to the structure's bottom could not be supported by the soil. You've got to be kidding. Sure enough we did find that the load bearing value of the soil was very low, surprisingly so, it probably couldn't have supported a big cow. Something was up here. I soon found out that the area was used under dire emergency conditions right after the great Baltimore fire at the turn of the 20th century to deposit all of the tons of ash and debris left by that almost city-wide conflagration.

Touché. The contractor led us down the Primrose Path. Somehow, he knew about the gigantic multi-acre wide ash dump in the area while we didn't and then suckered us in approval of a variation on our suggested concept design. He found a chink in our armor and was attempting to build a mountain out of a molehill, that would cost the State of Maryland $1,000,000. Remember this amount just so happened to be the exact amount the contractor's owner, who was good friends with the governor, needed to close his deal to purchase the Belvedere and make a killing on his gentrification contribution to once stately Baltimore, namely his condo conversion. How coincidental and very convenient it all was.

The only way I could beat this crook was to find out if he could have reasonably known that his very unusual choice of supporting a minor debris shield for the structure work above, that of building heavy steel support bent towers from the ground up, could have never worked as the ground was nothing more than thinly covered fire ash and debris.

But how?

So now, right on the heels of the Metro subway migrating gasoline fume fiasco, that cleaned out our budget, here comes a contractor, known to be real cozy with our governor who now claims an additional million dollars because, as the contractor rightly pointed out, he should have been able to assume that he could put cranes and other heavy construction equipment in the area because close by, an active railway line existed. Even considering the spread footing nature of a railroad ballast that widely dispersed the load, he had a good point. Something was a foot. Given that the site had been used and reused many times during the life of Baltimore, it was incumbent on him to perform a, "reasonable investigation into existing conditions." He provided a few select boring test results, wherein he drills holes down through the soil deep, that showed that he could expect good load bearing soil to be, but curiously these borings were few and far between and in odd locations, like they were a cherry-picked sampling of many taken and most likely he conveniently withheld those test soil borings showed something different than his desired narrative of good soil. I was suspicious now. I had to show that somehow, he knew of the ash dump that we had missed and he then exploited it in connection to us allowing him to support the temporary demotion shields from the ground. He had set us up and played us like a cheap violin. The connection between the million dollars for this and the million dollars needed to buy his hotel would have to be eventually made by the attorney general's office and the F.B.I. even if I got the goods on his nefarious scheme to defraud. But when all was said and done really, I could care less what happened to him or even the governor. That Contractor could steal his million dollars and even give his buddy, the governor, the best condo in his new Belvedere Hotel, I didn't care. I wanted to take down Taybeck only.

Chapter Three
The Meeting

Even though I worked for Harry for three years as one of his senior management team, providing recommendations that he learned to trust and rely on with no question given the time and effort limitations that he labored under, I had never been called into his office to explain, debate and otherwise detail my methods and findings regarding any construction claim I was charged in analyzing.

As this summons to the boss' office came right on the heels of being brought up to date by the clandestine passed off information I had received from that guy in the fine Italian suit on the street, this, in itself, further clued me in that something big and nasty was going down.

Harry was a big man, and a well fed one too. While not fat, he cast a wide shadow on a sunny day. He had thinning black hair that spoke of a shock of an uncontrollable mop top in his day. Owing to very bad myopia, he wore very thick lens glasses that magnified and put his lively, full of expression eyes on stage for everyone to read and know his most inner thoughts on any manner in real time. Suffice to say that Harry should have never played poker. He was the real deal though, worked his way up in the rough highway construction business, rough and tumble as it is, especially in the field out on the actual road.

When all was said and done though, he was a compassionate sort, parading as a rough around the edges no nonsense kind of guy, but a real teddy bear that could become and did become a Grizzly if need be.

Even though this meeting was ostensibly called for me to brief everyone on my findings, and I had carried in all my analysis, charts reports, calculations and such, we (me, my supervisor and his, like all government operations too many chiefs not enough Indians) all knew once the door closed, the fat would be well chewed about the contractor's known reputation, how it had markedly slipped in last several years and the widely now known (thanks to me not being able to keep anything secret unless under threat of punishment or just a polite clear request from the teller to keep mum) scuttle butt about the politics involved between the governor and his buddy contractor.

When the door was closed, Harry, behind his desk smiled the broadest smile I ever saw on him and his eyes twinkled and his eyebrows danced, all again magnified greatly by his coke bottle thick spectacles. (I can say this about Harry, with no reserve, as my glasses are just as thick.)

I short circuited the meeting regarding my review data, as I got the hint that was not in question, after all I had performed it twice, and it was checked by an outside consultant who arrived at an almost identical result as I had come up with, so I just plopped the now infamous manilla envelope with a ripped open corner from being overstuffed and its contents down in front of Harry, the very same way that my well-dressed 'deep throat' had given it to me. Come to think of it, how did this guy know I would be outside, across the street from our office building in front of the girly pole dancing bar, where our pre-designated fire drill gathering spot was… unless he knew a lot of our inner workings and possibly pulled the fire alarm, maybe it wasn't just a planned drill after all?

Harry picked up the envelope and took a good 15 minutes in silence to review. "Well, something sure stinks in Denmark and in the Great State of Maryland it seems," he said as he took his coke bottle bottom glasses off and rubbed his eyes. (Funny, when people who wear thick glasses like that take them off, their eyes then look so tiny like those of a mole, when they really aren't, but I digress. Good thing I wear contacts though, again I digress, sorry.) He then asked if the city guy had given me a head's up on any of this under belly stuff involving the governor and the contractor's close relationship. "Who was the city guy who pitched their claim?" he asked as well.

In a lightning strike of clarity, my head spun and I screamed inside as here, my boss, with his always intuitive spot on take on any issue, no matter how cluttered up, got right to the heart of the matter as far as I was concerned – Mr. Taybeck. Sure, it was very dramatic involving the governor and all that, but I just wanted personal revenge against Taybeck. This is my cross to bear, besides not ever being able to say no to any woman. I guess I have two crosses to bear concurrently, oh well.

My sole target, the reason now that I would beat this contractor and his sponsors, et al, like a rented mule, was to get Mr. Taybeck.

I filled Harry in on the pitch by Taybeck and as I proceeded to recount every slimy detail of our first meeting together, I could see Harry's gigantic eyes narrowed almost to slits and his brows slope inward. After a "humph," Harry said that Taybeck was a complete asshole, always was, always will be, a wannabe political hack. Never tested for any position, but always seemed to get the choiciest and after being thrown out of state government, immediately went to the city. I was giggling inside, wanted to tell how he was literally thrown out of his state office by John, who then unceremoniously picked him up and carried and dumped him in that third man's room stall , but I am not one to gloat.

Turns out Harry and Taybeck both attended the world renown Polly Technical Institute in Baltimore, the preparatory school for civil engineers. He said everyone knew Taybeck skated trough thanks to his daddy's money and influence. More political influence was at play to get him in than the old family's money though, as Taybeck's grandfather or great grandfather had lost most of that on some stupid scheme to develop some subprime land in the wilds of Georgia eons ago, by trying to drain a swamp by employing his original designed and patented cofferdam, instead of one that worked. The old man had one major potential buyer, a mill relocating from up north in Fall River Massachusetts. The story went that the great grandfather was the same, no account, lousy engineer that his grandson now is, this fool kept trying to build his crappy misguided designed cofferdam on grade for seven years straight until he went belly up financially. It broke the family. Harry relayed that he had once visited their big mansion in Roland

Park when he was a young man with Taybeck, and while outside it was quite impressive, inside it was an unequivocal dump, with relatives all around, even living in the basement on cots. There was no more old money and this loser current day Taybeck, that we were now having to deal with was, even though his dad scraped together enough to bribe his way to a state job, destined for mediocrity at best, a lowly civil servant on the take.

I could have kissed Harry for this intel on my true target, the one that now put white hot steel in my spine, a purpose in my every step, to crush that bug. My mind whirled, I really didn't hear too much more of the strategy of how we were to proceed, the plan to navigate this pollical 3rd rail that could end all our careers prematurely. The next thing I noticed was Harry, standing up, the air just from his movement stirring the papers wildly on his desk, and coming around front, sitting on the corner of his desk. At this point Harry pointed in my general direction and said, "We got to think." I should have really focused in on this, but as I knew who I was gunning for and why, I had a passion and that would carry me through, let me prevail, as it always had in the past, so my mind was free in creative idleness when Harry pointed and said, "We got to think."

As a result of my self-satisfied day dreaming while the boss was laying out his well thought out strategy to win, to beat the contractor and by the extension, the governor, the former mayor of Baltimore as well, I missed the battle plan altogether and because the last thing I heard him say was a variation on, "You Better Think", I was now picturing Harry, dancing seductively around the desk, all 6 foot 275 pounds of him, wearing an apron and long a blond wig, telling us, "You gotta think." My sincere apologies to the late, Ms. Aretha Franklin.

We ended the meeting with an order just to sit tight, no more work on the claim, and only communicate to the contractor or the city's Mr. Taybeck through Harry or the division chief, Thomas Grayson. Harry confided in us that he and Mr. Grayson had already met on the claim and more importantly he had shared the whole grimy backstory with the division chief although Grayson already knew of all the sordid delicious details thanks to my loose lips. Pretty good, I must say as that guy only gave me the goods three days earlier.

As I was leaving, Harry said that on second thought, he wanted me to run a whole new investigation of every detail supporting my findings and take a new tact in double checking my data and pursue it in all new avenues. Find out how the contractor knew the soil was bad even though trains pass through there on those tracks every day. "Be creative" is what he left me with "I heard you are a ham and do theatre, so creativity is right up your alley, in your toolbox as the enlightened like to say, right."

"Give it a fresh new look with new eyes if you can. No repeating your old ways and methods. Outside the box. Prove that he could have known, should have known even, that the soil was bad, the fill ash from the Baltimore Fire, even with the railway running through there and we can save the Belvedere from being condo—ized." With this Harry winked a five foot high wink giving his thick glasses and right there and then I knew where Harry's priorities were- saving that Grand Old Dame of a Hotel from being turned into a Yuppie Palace.

I decided to go to our archives in hopes of finding the truth, and if I could, then it goes to reason that the contractor could have as well. I had a chance to save the taxpayers a million bucks, while sticking my finger in the ultimate figure of authority's eye, namely the governor, along with the aging plastic G.I. Joe and as rebelling against any and all authority is part and parcel of who I am considering my past. "It was now on," as the kids say today.

Given that Baltimore was a major modern U.S. city immersed in the high-tech world in every way, the idea that their city's records archives were still in the hot attic of an old fire trap of a building a block from city hall was mind boggling. Penny wise and pound foolish I thought as I climbed amidst old metal and wooden plan racks in the morning summer 80-degree, high humidity, breath smothering heat in the block long ancient wooden structure.

While not the most prestigious of white-collar tasks, one that an engineer with the private sector might balk at and refuse to undertake, I was in public employment the same as my mother was as I already have told about and, therefore, my employment included the same infamous, all inclusive catch all phrase "all other duties as deemed necessary" as listed upon each and every of our job descriptions.

On this day, there was no white shirt or tie, no blazer, just an old 'Live Aid' washed out T-shirt and jeans with Adidas trainer shoes as replacement for wing tip dress shoes. I am what my doctor calls a 'Sweater.' I perspire profusely just changing a light bulb and sweat a deluge if swinging a hammer even in mild temperatures. (To be fair though, my doctor made this observation of me while he was about to perform my first prostate exam ever, I had to a right to sweat then.)

In this gigantic institutional cavernous attic, with humidity hovering around 80% and temperature around 100 F., I was leaving water droplets all over the archival construction as built plans that I had had finally located after an hour search and now was looking over. These plans had survived the hazards of decades and even a century, but now their fragile brittle paper and barely visible ink were being drenched in the sweat an amateur Sherlock Holmes wannabe.

This attic sauna foray into our archive was made by dodging roughly hewed wooden thick columns that were everywhere, by the light of a few bare bulbs as there were no windows. The wood was as old and in a similarly carved fashion that I remember seeing on a tour of the Post-Revolutionary War era frigate, The U.S.S. Constellation' now sitting retired in Baltimore Harbor.

Voila, I did locate the As-builts showing Penn Railway Station and the surrounding area as well as for the Bridge in question. Not in the plan drawers, but in a long wooden box along with several old glass bottles, mason jars I think they call them, filled with a black powdery, oily laced substance. By the time I schlepped the box down to the ground level from the 3rd floor and walked then the three blocks to my office that sat in a building katty corner from City Hall, my clothes were drenched. People stared, the guards stared, but as long as I had my photo ID taken when I was dry, and it looked somewhat like me, they let me back in the sweet 20th century air conditioning, dripping all the way, carrying what looked like a long very narrow wooden coffin for a snake.

Back in my office, I closed the door after saying good night to everyone, I stripped off my Live Aid Concert T-shirt to deal with the freezing air conditioning against my soaking wet skin.

Propped my feet up and typical of a pencil pusher after performing the slightest physical exertion, fell fast asleep.

With the workday over, and no phones, I slept soundly. Seven stories up it was as quiet as home some 40 miles away in the foothills of the Catoctin Mountains. At about 8:30 in the evening though, the cleaning people knocked on my door and woke me. They went away once told I was working late and no need to clean my office that Friday night. My shirt was all but dry now so I put it on as I was freezing and being half naked in the office late at night would put me in that special class of Office Don Juans if seen, although there was no fellow employee in there with me.

When I unrolled the ancient plans, more than century old, I heard them crinkle and snap, like the sounds I now made when waking up each morning since I am over 30 years old. Surprisingly, the paper didn't rip as there seem to be a cloth material interwoven in them or maybe the original 'pig skin' they used back then for diplomas and such. Looking down on the title sheet of the drawings I saw the signatures of the draftsmen and engineer, and took a long deep measured breath. They were long dead, never to worry about building things in the physical world again. Their company, Monumental Engineering is long gone. A sadness, a profound respect rushed over me like a wave. Finally, foolishly perhaps, I felt it necessary to send a prayerful hello and introduction to these fellow colleagues now in the afterlife and ask for their help and guidance in my review and search for the evidence that would crush the fraudulent claim and those who perpetrated it. On the surface the prayer sounded silly, but I was hedging my bet, hoping to not to have to bring a Ouija Spirit Board in should I get stumped and needed some answers from the now ghostly horse's mouth.

By 3:30 Saturday morning, I was up to speed as to the what, where, why and how Penn Station and the surrounding area came to be and this was important as the station was just north of the bridge. Even that the station was appointed with stain glass from the famous Tiffanys of New York. At the time, the station was the best built and most innovative in the world. Also, as I was hoping, shown on latter year updates was that all of the area immediately south of the station was a dump for the hundreds of thousands of tons of debris and ash generated by the great Baltimore fire and removed here to allow for the timely rebuilding of Baltimore.

In the vicinity of the claim involved area of work there is a railroad line, but as it runs through the Baltimore fire debris field – a gigantic fill area some fifty feet deep – the rail ballast area was built on steel piling that had been driven down through the unstable soil, debris and ash to the bedrock below... If I could find that information in one hot afternoon at the readily available to all archives, so could any contractor in their required preliminary investigation. The contractor hid his knowledge of how the railroad was supported in the area and feigned reliance on the presence of the tracks as a reason for him to believe all was normal with the soil. We have them by the "short hairs" I yelled across the barren empty offices. It wasn't so much as a lowly public engineer use to battling and often losing against teams of well-paid engineers and lawyers with unlimited resources at their disposal, although that was part of it, but more from my abusive childhood where long term cruelty and meanness were covered up by the corrupt and crooked powers to be that looked the other way. A fight for what was right while maybe a corny cliche was part of who I was now, for better or worse. I sat down completely exhausted and drained. Hunger drove me to raid all of the offices' refrigerators leaving many I.O.U.s in my scavenger wake.

All in all, it was quite a feast, thanks to the office microwave. After calling home and telling my mother that I was staying at Ruth's, my casual significant other for the past eight years, house over the week end again, a lie, but a well-intentioned white lie so she wouldn't worry, I sat down to really study the plans more in depth only to fall asleep again. This time no cleaning people woke me and I didn't wake until early evening, next day Saturday. The office carpet was thin, but enough to sleep on. Trying to get up I kicked one of the bottles from the archive over that contained the black gunk, that was no longer a mystery as to content or reason they were saved. The engineer who updated the original plans a few years after the railway was installed on piles throughout the area had included the contents of the sample boring coring material then taken. That black stuff was old, incinerated, ash, small chips of mortar, oil and tar, as well as the remains of a few unlucky and slow horses, mules, cows, dogs, cats and even a few people who didn't out run or were too drunk to get out of the way of the blazing town wide inferno. I once talked to an old timer who lived in Jarrettsville some 30 miles north of Baltimore and he remembered as a young boy seeing the glow in the sky from the fire from his front porch. In the jars were also a few coins from the 1830s on up to 1892 that had the edges melted and disfigured from the intense heat. After scooping all of spilled contents back into the bottle, I couldn't help thinking what the cleaning people would think caused the carpet to be ruined there, and it smelled just awful. As I finished putting the last of oily ash into the bottle, my vision went from color to black and white than all black. The last thing I felt was my head hit the pile of soft old plans spread across my desk.

As I came to, not but a few minutes later at best, the cold florescent office lights above were now a single warm, sparkling flickering light in a crystal-clear light bulb, throwing dancing shadows across my eyes and the plans.

Somewhere very near I could hear muffled argumentative male voices and drawers being slid opened and slammed closed. And heavy walking and rolling sounds above on an uncarpeted wooden floor just above my head. At first, I thought maybe this was Mercy Hospital a few blocks away and the light, that of an examination room, but no one was around. No bright hospital lights no whiteness, just darkness, like looking through thick, opaque glass. A door slammed loudly with, "Find those plans or we'll all get terminated on Monday!" yelled very loudly.

Then silence. Then rustling for about 1/2 of an hour, then the sound of closing old-fashioned windows shut, whirling chains, followed by the tramping of two sets of shoes going down creaky wooden steps and another door silence. There were no windows or steps on the floor above my office, and most likely not in Mercy Hospital's emergency room either, so where was I?

The Penn Station archive drawings and boring data sheets were now atop what looked like a very large steamer trunk and I was no longer in my small carpeted office, but sitting on a stack of wooden crates in a large dark room with pipes and old fashion twisted power cables running everywhere. There were steps over in the corner next to a big, cast-iron circular thing. With no idea of anything I got up and went toward the steps, next to the steps was a furnace of some sort and I could smell wet coal. There was a string hanging down almost to the floor at the base of stairs. I pulled it or rather an object tied to it and two crystal clear glass bulbs, very round flickered on. Just like the other, you could see the filaments inside burning brightly. I went up the stairs and opened the door that had the old kind of enamel white knobs that yuppies all kill for to put in their homes now. It was dark inside but, to the right there was a large window with an orange like glow coming in from the street. Written backward in a wide arch across the expansive window was "Monumental Engineering Consultants. Baltimore, Chicago and San Francisco." On the wall, between the rather plain residential style front wooden door and the big front window hung a wall calendar with pictures of the Holy Land on it where all the dates had big black x's through from June 1 through, and including Tuesday, June 8, so I deduced that this was the night of June eighth, but the year caused me to shudder, 1909. The last thing I could remember from the office was it was Friday, June 9, 1989, so I had gone back in the week three days and back in the century eighty years and one day. My head started to whirl, so I made my way back downstairs to the refuge of the wooden pallets and wet coal smell and went to sleep or something that reasonably passed for sleep.

Some noises, even those not loud, but faint soft ones can sometimes wake you with a startle more so than an outside explosion. Such was the case as with the hallway grandfather's clock upstairs in the old fashion office; when it rang, it counted at every hour mark, waking me at 11:00 p.m., 1:00 a.m. and 3:00 in the morning. Now wide wake, or was I, I decided to play along not really wanting to, and explore my new world in every nook and cranny, like a cat in his new home. What could be the worst that would happen? That I would wake up from this elaborate dream. It was pitch black upstairs aside from the yellow glow coming from the street through that big front window. Automatically, I grabbed my cell phone, and although it had no signal, the blue light from its blank screen was enough to see about.

As a kid in Baltimore, we too had the same wooden sloping outside basement barn like doors that I now lifted only one of to go out into the back outside area. Other than one small rectangle of light about 50 feet away on the second floor of a neighboring building or house, it was as dark as ink. However, looking straight up, it was dizzying, causing me to spin a little. The last time I saw a night sky like this, (so filled with stars that it would be more accurate to describe it as being full of sporadic black dots on a background of brilliant white than white stars shining in a black background) was when I a fourteen year old boy scout, high in the Rocky Mountains, hiking and camping far away and above anywhere or anyone.

The air though was not in complete concert with this glorious display of the heavens in all their expansiveness. The inky black of this night couldn't completely mask the unpleasant marks of man. Each yard had an outhouse and it seemed so in the middle of that hot summer night, enough said. Who knew flies swarmed at night? Although, waves of tiredness were coming again, maybe there was some sort of a form of Jet lag involved with time travel, if in fact, that is what this was and not just a particularly vivid dream, I didn't want it to go, as if it was only a dream, it was quite detailed, beautiful and wholly overwhelming to my senses on all fronts and something in me, didn't want to let it go. The constant flutter of clothes on clothes lines in the summer night breeze as far as I could see in the almost pitch dark, was lulling me to sleep and I knew I couldn't risk sleeping outside and being discovered there in the morning, if this was all real.

Before stealthily sneaking back in the basement with the help of a neighboring dog who had stopped barking and now was just satisfied to study me with an almost imperceptible low whine and sniffing, providing a directional orientation, (I never met a dog that didn't soon like me with the reverse being true as well), I looked up to drink it all in, not only what was above but around me too, one more time, if this was a dream after all. At first it didn't seem out of place and didn't catch my notice even , but there in the freckled white blazing against the dark night sky were the familiar red and white blinking lights of a passing aircraft above, although I could hear no jets or prop engines, it fit right in. But if this was in fact way back then what the hell was that doing here. I watched the lights until they disappeared off in the distance. My head hurt; it was swimming from the thoughts I was trying to now comprehend. This all was so disjointed I must be deep asleep. I pinched myself and felt it good, I was stone cold awake. What they say about our arms being too short to box with God is true. What would be would be. There was no controlling this scenario and in a strange, reassuring way, that brought me some comfort, I whispered, "Good night" to my new furry friend next door, and went in and crashed into a deep, instantaneous slumber on top of my pile of plans now serving double duty as a miniature thin mattress on top the cool, stone floor. As I drifted quickly off to the Land of Nod though, I had time to wonder if this basement, with its loose stone floor with many open seams, was ever tested for radon.

Chapter Four
Meeting People

Was this little girl's intent to tie me up with the rope and, if so, how brave she must be?

Terrified inside, I lay motionless though as she walked round and round me as I lay on the basement floor seemingly still fast asleep.

As I could see her rope was short and yellow and blue, I relaxed a bit as it was for jumping and not restraining. "Are…are…are…you playing possum, mister?" I stayed motionless, eyes almost all closed. Or, or, or did you just get drowned? My heart stopped. Maybe I was now dead as I thought I might be all last night when I wasn't thinking I was sleeping and this was the answer for all this, and she was the first angel I've thus to meet. She lightly put the end of her rope on my head and then pulled it along my whole body. I twitched and she jumped back.

The jig was up. "Hello little angel, and what is your name?"

We stared at each other for a minute or two and she said, "You first."

I sat up and she moved back a bit, and then said, "Well, don't you all know these things, when we are coming, our names and stuff." She just kept staring, I was confusing her now as well as scaring her. "I just mean doesn't Saint Peter give you guys a memo or something to update you."

When I said 'St. Peter' she smiled and said, "You-you-you're Catholic too."

Oh, geeze, an angel that stutters, but I didn't say it out loud.

Did you-you drown too? What the hell, look at your update, I don't know what happen. She started to cry. This sure wasn't heaven.

"I'm sorry, it's just that I'm tired. Why do you think I drowned?" After a bit, she looked at me and said that she could see the wall through me, like a ghost, just like her mother had seen in her Uncle Randy after he fell through the ice and died. I checked and yes in spots, I was a bit transparent, the effect was coming and going, like a fluttering.

"I don't feel dead, but don't you know if I am or not little angel."

"I'm not an angel, I am Esther Owens and am 7½ years old and live at 512. Ex-Exe-Exeter Street, apartment c." That matched the street sign I saw through the window upstairs last night. Some sanity now.

"Well, hello Esther. My name is James. Mr. Morrison and I live on Mayberry Road in Westminster, Maryland."

"Where is-is that?"

Not thinking I replied, "About 40 miles away."

"Did you take the tra-tra-train all that way?"

"No, I drove and then took the Metro."

She just stared and said that I talked and smelled funny.

"Miss Esther, can you keep a secret? I don't know how I got here or really what is happening."

"But don't bi-big people know everything there is?"

"Most times we do, but other times we don't."

She laughed at this and said her ma, mom, mommy and da, da daddy knew everything.

"Are you here for the job Daddy wants someone to do?"

Well, after an hour or two of this give and take, little Esther let me know that they lived on the third floor of the building we were now in and her father was the draftsman for the Monumental Engineering Company in Baltimore. His name was Joseph Owens, his real name is Daddy or Joe she said, and her mother was named Mommy or Katy or Catherine.

I told the little girl that I was lost in the city and just came in to sleep and bless her kind heart, she accepted that as a matter of course, no more questions.

"Do you want to see my dollhouse daddy made for me?" We got up and went to the back of the large, stark bare area I was in. Over in the corner on some wood resting between the seats of two hard back chairs, was a blue little structure. As she explained each tiny piece of furniture and whose room it came from, I stretched my neck to peek out the high small windows. It was raining hard and I could see the drops bouncing back into the air from the window frame base. Outside there was a cluster of small buildings in a long line, all wood, everything wood, fences too. They were privies, out houses. This most certainly was not heaven. I heard a rhythmic slapping noise and looked back down to see Esther jumping rope furiously. She seemed mad. I was talking to you, and all you can do is look out that window. I apologized profusely to Esther and took note that she hadn't stutter at all while jumping rope.

Upstairs somewhere the sound of foot falls coming down steps and a deep, bass voice calling, "Esty, come here. Can you help Daddy look for something?"

She dropped rope and started to run to the stairs turning around to me saying, "Mums the word, Mr. Morrison, don't bother Daddy 'till they open the office up, he's all mine until then, I put my finger to my lips," and she giggled and bounded up the stairs.

After a half an hour or so, someone was coming down, and I ducked around the coal furnace and waited to get caught, at 6'2" with a shock of red hair and no grace on my feet, I could never hide. It was Esther with a canvas bag. She ran right to where I was hiding and said, "I ga-ga-got you, you're the counter and seeker now."

I always was the lousy counter/seeker in that game. She handed me a canvas bad with some apples, soda crackers and a jar of preserves or jelly, (I never knew the difference between the two) and said I must be quiet as her father was going to be in the office upstairs. She said that the old pump pipe thing in the basement door room might still work for water then bounded back up the steps. My 7-year-old mother- eighty-seven in my time. The crackers were terrible, the preserves fantastic and the apples were apple-ish. I found the basement door room. In reality it wasn't a whole room, only the area outside the basement vertical door covered by the two large sloping doors to the outside as I did the night before, but when you are such a little girl, I guess it qualified as a room. Five brick steps were in between the sloping doors and the doorway opening in the basement wall with a small flat area landing at the bottom. Right smack dab in the center, preventing anyone from really using this entrance unless they were small like Esther, was a vertical cast iron black pipe, with an old pump handle, although the metal was bright as brand new. I have no idea how I missed walking into that last night when going out and coming back that way, maybe I was less physical more atmospheric then. Slowly I pumped water out and took a shower of sorts. It took some time for the drain to empty then, making sure it was well washed out as I believed this was the little girls 'secret room.'

I heard a young women's voice filter down through the furnace grate upstairs. It was light but had a very heavy German accent.

She said, "Joseph, I am not a pack mule and if you keep this up, our family will never grow."

Then a male voice saying, "Ready.1,2,3," and then the most God-awful scraping sound and a series of bangs and a sound like marbles falling. I was about to instinctively blow my cover as my imagination immediately told me that he was murdering both of them, an ingrained snap conclusion I brought back from 1989 Baltimore. As I reached for the basement banister though, I heard Esty's voice, float around melodically saying, "I got them, Pappa, I can reach them."

From my brief reconnaissance expedition the night before, I calculated that where they all were at the big drafting table right in front of the offices bay window with the firm's name on it. Odd place to place a drafting table, but I guess it was supposed to have advertisement value, give an air of prestige and professionalism. I then heard

Joseph say, "No, they aren't the station plans, but the War Memorial Building side steps."

Dead quiet, then Catherine asked Esty to go upstairs. once she was gone, she said, "Did he really say you were gone if you couldn't find them by Monday?"

All Joseph said in reply was "that they have to be here. else they were stolen by those Bradley folks." I was familiar with the name Bradley as they were now one of the biggest engineering consultants throughout all of Maryland...that is they will be in 1989. Maybe I was sent here to help find the missing plans, now it was getting interesting. As I set on my pile of crates cushioned by the Penn Station Plans that I had somehow brought with me, I was ready to hear more of this adventure. But then, as always happens in my life when I am in deep trouble, the actual cause of the trouble, I felt ice water in my veins. Looking between my man spread as I sat, a thunderclap of the obvious occurred to me. I had brought the very same plans that Joseph was now frantically searching for to save his and his family's livelihood.

I heard muffled cries from above, not of Catherine's, but they were of a man – Joseph's. If this were a Hallmark Channel tear Jerker TV show, I would now rush upstairs and save the day, but it wasn't that simple. Yes it was real and I could have done that, but I am a coward and was frozen with fear. He would think maybe I stole them, and copied their innovated designs as they really were in that day, and Bradley would now somehow steal the account from them. Everybody went up to the third floor where the little family lived as Esty had told me earlier, three very slow climbing pairs of feet, so unlike the floating, skip like bounding of the little female sprite only a few moments earlier.

With nothing to do, I unrolled the plans and as I always did when plans of anything technical were around, I lost myself in them. Some say it's a detriment, but I have always been able to single mindedly focus on plans and specifications to the exclusion of all of the outside world, for hours at a time, with no break. The plans were innovative and bordered on elegance, there were the stained-glass plates from Tiffany's Company of New York to be placed around the perimeter of the roof edge. I did take the liberty to add notes here and there, dated and initialed my changes out of habit. Add rubber flanges where plates are attached to minimize breakage from the nearby train vibrations, increase fall of sewage drain from first floor. Provide sturdier hangers for the main train schedule board to compensate for live load of worker updating board while on board catwalk, etc.

When I came back to my senses, a clock tower somewhere outside was chiming five o'clock in the evening. I long ago stop wearing a watch as my constant staring looking down at it even while talking to my bosses, got me in trouble. The bad side of having a type A personality. And guess what, my flip cell phone while still having almost a full charge, didn't provide the time as it now couldn't find a signal, go figure. Now there was noise from the back outside, people walking down steps. No wonder there aren't as many fat people in this time than mine, all the stair walking. Again peeking out the high little rectangle window in the basement, I waited and finally saw all three of my housemates, Esty, her mom and dad. Esty with her curly brown hair and pretty red dimples led while her parents, he handsome in a way of angular bone structure and her mother, rather plain, but with a peaches and cream complexion that radiated in the low sun now that the rains had stopped. They were all dressed up, he in a suit and tie, blue dresses for mother and daughter and hats all around and black shoes on all as if they were going to the church as, in fact, they were. Esty ran up to a barn like structure across the little alley and pulled a rope that traveled up to the second floor of the building and rang a big rusty cowbell. Hanging from a big nail. While the parents waited a little black boy's head appeared from between the large square doors where I think they get hay in. I heard, "Ahoy, Esty," from the little guy to which Esty replied,

"It is Esther or Miss Esty, never just Esty. We're going to Mass now, and I wanted to know if you wanted me to say a prayer for you and your mother."

The boy, nodded in the affirmative, then greeted the parents with, "Hello Mr. Joseph, Miss Catherine, sure glad the rain stopped."

"Hello to you, Solomon, say Hi to your mother and remember I got that second book, Huck Finn, when you finish with Master Sawyer." The boy replied he was midway through the book, but would hurry now as he wanted to read about Huckleberry Finn and the Mississippi river rafting so very bad.

By me somehow taking the "As-Built" station plans from the Baltimore City archives yesterday morning in 1989, this act now made the construction plans that this firm had poured their hearts and souls into, just disappear here in 1909. Not really though, I had them just a few feet away downstairs. After thinking, really more like just sitting vacant headed waiting for an answer to come to me of what to do, (which usually served me pretty well in arriving at solutions for difficult problems like this – I chalk up these divine solutions as coming from my late older brother, Tom, who always had the answers, if you could only bear to hear him out given his slow, deliberate manner of speech) Tom's answer came through, some forty years before he would even be born. Guess in Heaven time does not exist after all.

The answer: just take the plans upstairs and leave them there, hide them like they were there all along. Another incoming divine flash: First rip off the title sheet final signed signature blanks and remove and post construction notes, addenda, red and green line changes that had been added by me and others over the past 80 years. It took some time of just blotting over the changes rather than trying to erase them.

It was about 30 minutes later when I placed the redacted As Built Plans as I knew them to be way in the future, now only the preliminary construction plans of the Penn Station as Joseph and his colleagues now knew them to be, in a very ugly Spanish looking, brightly colored umbrella stand by the office front door and draped someone's coat I had found in the closet over the top. Pretty good touch, if I say so myself. After studying the office intently for some time it looked more like a captain's ship cabin with all the polished wood everywhere, than a stuffy work-a-day salt mine. After playing with the wall gas jets that weren't used for light any longer given the bare, ornate shaped see-through fancy electric bulbs everywhere, I thought it best to go back downstairs to my quarters in the basement or was it called a cellar back then. As I headed down, I passed a paper calendar on the inside of the basement door. It had pictures of French "Can- Can" girls on it, so that's why it was on the inside of the door. On Thursday, June 10, marked in a bold engineer's style block printing was a note: "Final Presentation of Specs and Plans for Penn Station to B & O and Baltimore City officials." Just in the nick of time. The small family were returning home from Church and climbing the outside stairs. The Cavalry now retired to his crates down below. The not-so-hideous to have to don a partial mask, albeit a very stylish one, phantom of the basement/cellar.

Next morning, I awoke to coffee, eggs and sausage sat in a wooden bucket by Miss Esty and her friend from across the alley, young Solomon. It was like looking at a preteen version of Louis Armstrong. Solomon had that same infectious smile of the famous ambassador of goodwill, only in miniature, but the lankest, skinniest body of anyone I have ever saw. Healthy, but ready for a growth spurt any second, like we all did in my family.

"Good morning to you, Mr. Morrison. My name is Solomon, and I live across the way and am friends with all the Owens family, but mostly only with Esty, I mean Miss Esty. Don't worry none though, we both swore to keep you a secret unless you are an escape convict and then we will only tell after you are long gone."

I was stunned, what unreserved kindness, tears wanting to stream down my face, but I didn't want to upset these kids. Speechless. Solomon took the food out of bucket and sat it out, in little tin plates, shallow bowls really, on the floor, then gave me a spoon. Before I could say thanks, he apologized for not being a very good cook and not having a napkin. All I could muster in reply was a soft thank you.

While I ate, Solomon and Esty both played with the doll house pretending to be immersed in it while dashing furtive glances my way.

Telling the children that I had been sick and now forgetful and lost seemed to satisfy their curiosity and as well their fears. Why not, they were still innocent in a more innocent time, where people didn't expect everyone to lie like rugs.

Solomon was fascinated by my clothes and the way I talk, "used a lot of funny words" as he said. He asked me about the outline of Africa on my shirt and what did 'live aid, mean.' Although he pronounced it as, to live not that it was broadcast live like on satellite worldwide television. I just passed it off as some artwork that a friend did, saying to live in Africa is definitely an aid to living well. He smiled broadly, ear to ear, believing this rotten liar, but what could I do, I ask you?

Also, he said my shoes looked like canvas sailor shoes, only that they were instead blue and had the word 'ADIDAS' written on them. He asked if that was my first name, to which Miss Esty jumped in with knowing authority saying, "No, his first name is James."

Then young Solomon guessed again, "Is it your middle name?"

I said, "No, my middle name is Allan. Like Edgar Allan Poe."

He said, "I Give up."

I just said, "Yup." He giggled at the way I said 'yup.' "That man was one of my favorite writers." He said his was

Mark Twain. We were talking up a storm. I didn't let on that my favorite works, were Sam Clemens' darker ones like the *Mysterious Stranger* so as not to pollute his boyhood joy of Tom Sawyer and Huck Finn in any way. He mentioned he was about to read *Huckleberry Finn*, something I already knew from eaves dropping in on his conversation in the alley with Esty and her parents the night before.

He dropped a bomb then that left me dizzy and excited. He shared that his boss knew the night guard at that new big hotel up on Charles Street and that early next week, Mr. Twain himself will be in the city, staying there overnight. It was supposed to be private, but it got out.

Miss Esty was fidgeting, jealous of our now boys only inclusive conversation. I stopped and said, "Miss. Esty, I have got a real big surprise for you." Her eyes lit up, and then closed with her little hand instinctively extended out, fingers wiggling. When I told her that I hid it upstairs in the umbrella stand near the door under a coat, she, as always when happy it seemed, bounded away, skipping up the steps, in double time this time though.

I heard rustling, Solomon and I held our collective breaths. A squeal. Then out of nowhere she appeared with the missing plans, as big as her in her hands. She kissed me, hugged me, did the same to Solomon and back up the stairs. I yelled keep it our secret. You be the hero all by yourself, ok? She replied, "cross my heart". Then Solomon, with my dirty dishes all in his bucket, looked at me, and with the wisdom of the ages said, "Mr. Morrison, you are a good man, and my new friend."

"Out of the mouths of babes", a truer statement never applied better. He left by the basement door and I watched him go in the barn building. Right there and then, I knew that both Solomon and I would be in the presence of one Samuel Clemens, a.k.a. Mark Twain, at the "New" Belvedere Hotel in just a matter of days. This was our combined, mutual fate of two people born some sixty years apart, but in the same place.

We, Miss Esty, Solomon and I spent the entire afternoon talking and talking and talking. For Solomon it was his only day not working a twelve-hour day and for Esty she was home alone all afternoon after her patents were invited to the prestigious 'Engineers Club' near the Washington Monument and Peabody Conservatory to a pre-construction party and dinner, along with his boss, for the new Penn Station building as guests of the construction company's chief engineer, all arranged in a very rushed, last-minute fashion once the plans were found.

We don't play much with the other children around here since they all the time tease Solomon and call him awful names, only because he told him about having that dream of his over and over again where this older black man says that little children will one day live where they will not be judged by the color of their skin, but by their how they live. They all do it too just because his skin is dark, no one makes fun of them because they're ugly and smell, because they do, especially the boys. The world according to Esty that hot summer afternoon as I tried to get this little wooden barrel to flip up on a peg, a toy of Solomon's that was really the devil's work as far as I was concerned. Funny thing though as long as I kept trying to get the thing to work and all the while Esty watched me, she didn't stutter at all. I hated that wooden barrel peg thing, worse even than those god-forsaken rubik's cubes to come along in seventy years.

"Andrew looks just like a horse face and Charles even has chip munk teeth and they still can play out front."

"I tried to yell at them, but they call me Eth-thie…Eth-thie… Eth-thie…making fun of my stuttering. I hate them." For a pint size little gal, Miss Esty sure had a quart size spine.

You know Esty that someday colored people in our country will just be called African-American as so will Italian-Americans, Irish-Americans, German-Americans that come here and have "American" added to the end of the country that they or their parents or grandparents came from before coming here.

I am going to let you know of something said by a very great man. This guy, I mean man did, I mean, will cause the world to change not by using any Army or Navy, but by his lone example of the way he lived, full of peace and not fighting back even in the face of all sorts of meanness and cruelty against him and what he was trying to accomplish. By doing just so, his way was so different, so new that even the dumbest of all stupid men eventually saw how wrong and mean they were and out of place in God's world where this man happily lived. Both Solomon and Esty piped in in unison, "We know it's Jesus…we do go to Sunday school."

I replied, "Great guess, but this man will be just like us, a regular American person, wearing shoes instead of sandals and a coat, but more like Solomon here because he will have a gigantic heart, a winning broad smile and his skin will be beautifully dark, just like Solomon's." The teen boy stood a little straighter and Esty grabbed his hand tight, tossing her head back and looking up at him proudly. What this great man said was that someday he knew that all men, women and children wouldn't be judged by the color of their skin any longer but only by the content of their character, just like Solomon here keeps dreaming about. I can't tell you why, but Solomon's dream is so very true and will be, honest Injun. They both howled when I, an adult, said things like that, that only kids say usually.

I can't tell you his name, not because I can't remember it, I just can't say that's all. It's is not my place, do you understand? Solomon shook his head while Esty moved hers from side to side, not understanding. Trust me though, you both will come to know his name when you are all grown up, I just feel it. To this Esty said, "Oh, another of those adult things that are kept from children." No Esty, no other adults even now know, except me. They both looked at each other than back to me. And I guess I only know because I have such great loving friends like you two, so maybe God knows I always will try to stay good and keep secrets for him, like I do for them. Only telling you two this one, since I think I am supposed too.

You two will have to trust me that all these things will come to past, that meanness and bullies like those kids out front will be made fun of someday themselves until they see it is wrong and just hurtful and hopefully change of their own accord. Making the right choices in this grand test called 'life.'

Look at it this way, you and Essy are already far ahead of them in the school of life. They are all still in 1st grade, and you two are close to graduating high school.

Esty was laughing at this. She said in real school she was now in 2nd grade for real.

I always knew how to pick the best of friends, both of you so smart, kind, and pretty, as I hugged Esty, and handsome to boot giving Solomon a shoulder tug. From his deep, thoughtful stare I gathered that Solomon understood a lot more of what I was talking about than the little girl. They both instantly returned to the happy, carefree world shining through in that moment once I hugged and tickled them, giggling together in the sweetest chorus.

Other than Esty's doll house there were no games to keep us busy aside from that cursed barrel and peg thing that the kids could both do again and again, but not me.

I thought some and said, "I just made up a brand-new game that I will call, call… called Trivial Pursuit 1909 (so I or my airs, if I ever got serious with Ruth back home a.k.a. Red, couldn't ever be sued in anyway by the actual developers of this game far in the future to come – I have no class) and I'll show you guys how to play, I mean young man and young lady."

Fine deal, my game and I lost to these kids. Who knew the categories would be Bible passages, types of horses, doll names, and train schedules?

As is their nature, when given her a chance to talk, she did with all the animation and joy that only children of single digit age have, she went on and on sharing her world, most generously sharing every detail of her young life the same as she would share the most precious rubies and diamonds, without hesitation, little making the distinction between daily events and gems, the former being as precious, if not more, than the latter. A smart little girl that knew this truth all along which adults don't learn often to a ripe old age. Between her exuberance to share and her stammering though, folks that were impatient as a matter of their pomposity, missed her spirit charged, nurturing talk. The whole while I was there, she alternately wore only two different homemade dresses, all that she had I guess. One, a blue checkered of calico material and the other a red and white one. With both she had what looked like an adult apron, but child size, that had a small pocket with a ribbon loop in the front that tied down her left forearm with her hand immovably secured fast in the pocket. My mind raced to polio or some injury that due to the times, became a permanent crippling one. She must have saw me staring sadly, as she then giggled and pulled her left hand out and shook both hands in the air freely. Then I even thought maybe it was a current style, a salute to Napoleon or something to do with modesty. It was none of those. She told me that her parents and teacher and even pastor were trying to get her to stop using her left hand as it was bad, a "Mark of the Devil" her grandma even once said that had to be overcame. She said she only pulled her hand out of the ribbon loop when adults weren't around or her best friend Solomon who wanted her to get better and be pious so she could be happy and play with him in heaven someday, even around white people. I looked at Solomon and he was smiling proudly, however, as he looked at my face, he stopped. My deep sadness at what she said could not be hidden.

Solomon was an honest boy as they come and then some with a deep moral compass that would make any parent, preacher or angel envious. A boy with a baby face with a full-grown Louis Armstrong smile. He was around 13 or 14, and although he, at one time was fortunate as a black child to have gone to school and could read and write, his father, who had worked for the B & O railroad at their Baltimore Roundhouse, thereby providing his family with a modicum of decency in home and diet, had died horribly in a train car coupling accident. From how Solomon heard it, It wasn't horrible as to pain, as his dad felt none, when his midsection was crushed when the couplings of two separate railway cars closed on him, but as to anguish, it was terrible because he was left fully conscious, standing impaled between the cars, but all the while knowing he would leave this earth, his love ones, his life, the moment the train cars were pulled apart. The supervisor had dealt with this horror twice before, it was not a freak accident back then, but an occasional, expected "cost of doing business" then, long before OSHA.

Solomon's father, Elijah, was just standing there in the bright afternoon sun, the sounds of the day all around. The rhythmic clanging of a hand rung outside school bell summoning the students back inside after lunch, the steam hissing from the two locomotives waiting to go into the round house and the soulful barking of a lone dog that may not, like most everyone else outside the walls of the rail yard, been oblivious to the private, localized, tragedy that was cruelly unfolding

The railroad supervisor calmly issued orders in such a matter-of-fact way, that it was clear this was not his first time dealing with such a unique, tragedy. He was sharing some whiskey and his pipe with Elijah, which in itself showed the extraordinary gravity of the situation as the supervisor was white and Solomon's father not. His fellow workers there that afternoon all would come up, one by one, said their private goodbyes and with a handshake or after gently patting him on his back slowly, then stoically exited, but when not in earshot, out of view behind the train cars they wailed and sobbed in sadness, some falling to the ground, others in the passenger car prone with their hands over their faces. At one point, Elijah and the supervisor were even laughing together, causing anyone who didn't know and may have just been passing by, to believe that all was well, even better than well. Sadly, this was not true as if they had looked more closely, between the red, now drenched rags put there to slow the bleeding, you could see one of Elijah's ribs sticking out over the metal edge of the coupling device. About two in the afternoon, a nun could be seen escorting Elijah's wife Emma, up the tracks with Solomon, then five years old in tow. Father, Michael, was not to be found, so they brought the Mother Superior of Elijah's family's parish for his last rights. It was then so quiet, not even the birds. It was odd to hear Latin come from such a high, shrill voice and not Father Michael's deep resounding, theatrical at times, one. There was more silence, a handshake from the supervisor, a hug and kiss from Emma and his son, who she was half clutching. his bare feet wiggling like he was dropping, then an air whistle from somewhere, the sound of metal clanging then Elijah silently slumped to the ground in a lifeless pile where once a man had just stood and lived.

Solomon who would talk up blue streak, didn't say a thing for months. Emma's mother said that she should not have let the boy see such a thing, but as an only child, she had no choice to bring him. And in her heart, Emma thought she had no right to keep Solomon from saying goodbye or denying her husband the same thing to his only son.

The little family scraped by mostly from the pittance of cash given by the railroad in such situations to the family, which was further reduced in an under-board way, by one third as Elijah was a black man.

Emma had family in South Carolina where she was from and they would send clothes and food by railway free, a perk the railroad allowed after the Baltimore Sun News Paper suggested it, knowing her extended family had a farm. Solomon continued in school until he was ten when the compassion and interests to sponsor the family, by the Baltimore elite faded and was no longer in vogue. His voice did come back, but first as a stammer and kids being kids, even black ones like the ones that populated Solomon's school # 28 for colored children, teased him unmercifully.

When society's largess withered away with their interest, their need to be conspicuously caring, coupled with the relentless teasing the boy got on a daily basis at school, Emma pulled her son out of school. Almost immediately Solomon got an apprenticeship with a blacksmith named Simon, who had his shop and livery stable right behind the row house containing the office of Monumental Engineering consultants on the first and second floors and Esty's and her parents' living quarters on top, the third story.

Children still trailing remnants of the sublimity of heaven, are noble by nature until shown and taught otherwise. Young Esther and Solomon would play together for hours on end in the evening after school, with chores for the little girl and hard physical labor for Solomon. Solomon would read the books Esther would bring him from the house and Esty would then listen more than talk, though Solomon never seemed to mind her stuttering, she could sometimes see him wince and stare away when she tried to talk in long sentences. They would be inseparable until darkness came. While the other children in the neighborhood would sometimes stay out later, bathed in the gas streetlight out front, playing hide and seek, these two, relegated to the dark alley between their homes by society's-imposed exile due to race and disability, did not have that luxury.

Chapter Five
Making a Call and Calling Upon

As to what holiday it may have been, none came to my mind for that time of year, at least ones that existed back then in my time, not even the many religious, Catholic ones, therefore, it was a mystery to me why the office upstairs was closed that weekday morning. All that the wall calendar up there on the back of the basement door noted was "All out of office full am" it could have been field work for the whole crew. They would be back for lunch, so I had to move quickly as it was already 10:30 a.m. At home in the 21st century, I never slept later than 8:00 o'clock, it must be something like Jet Lag, only affecting the perception of time passage – "time lag," yeah that must be it.

I opened the door slowly, while sitting on the top basement step peering out of the very bottom of the opening, that way if somebody was in there and happened to look at the space caused by the door now being slightly ajar, they would be less likely to see anyone as I was down at floor level, a trick I once saw in a movie. No one was out there, just the ticking of the grandfather clock, no receptionist, no assistant, no intern (as they didn't employ that back door method of free slavery labor back then as yet). Now to put my plan, that I had only quite vividly dreamt of only last night, into action.

But where in the hell is the phone, I know I kept hearing a ring? A tinny, weak, muffled ring, but an electronic cause ring nonetheless, not like waving a bell. Also, those loud one-sided conversations I so often heard drifting down to my basement hideout, muffled yet not informal, kind of presentational and stuffy, one-sided, going on every time right after the ringing let me know that they had a new-fangled telephone on remises. They would, I guess, being a professional business. It was most definitely a phone ring, maybe only an electric doorbell, damn. It wasn't a doorbell though, I hope it wasn't anyway, although it sounded just like one. The old kind, battery powered.

Now it was already twenty of eleven, where is it? Not on any desks, not even in the boss' office, not on any walls like they use to hang them. Nowhere. Where would I hide, if I was a boxy looking big ugly contraption that you talk into a voice cone and listen with another separated earpiece, that is if Hollywood had got it right for that era. After an extensive search, even though all the desk drawers, just as I was about to give up and run back downstairs or even outside to try to find the address of whom I wanted to then talk to in person, I saw a round roughly made hole about five inches in diameter drilled into one of the wall's oaken panels at waist level. Bet this is it. Just as I put my hand in the hole the very familiar ringing sound had started to sound from somewhere behind the wooden wall panel. Short intermittent rude unpleasant sounding bursts then silence. The wall slid back, like they all did in that old Scooby Doo cartoon, like a mini pocket door into the adjacent wall. Here it was, the contraption was just as I imagined it except very shiny with thick varnish over it, it almost looked like plastic imitation wood, Hollywood got it right. They had an old bar stool in the tiny room closet, a fore runner to a telephone booth, (funny this was before the telephone booth and the time I came from was just after them as cell phones made them all obsolete. The only thing they were then good for was for the homeless using them for outdoor bathrooms, no more calls ever to be answered in them, but for the call of nature-sorry that was bad). Sitting on the bar stool, I left the panel opened so I could hear if anyone was coming, took a breath and picked up the ear sound piece. Dead as a door nail. Damn, then I remembered reading that the telephone systems were down more than they were up back in this time before the bugs were all ironed out. I was again about to give up when I realized the brass metal on the side of the phone was a crank, aha, now I knew what to do, this was how you started it, by cranking it, just like the cars would have to have done to start them in that time.

That did it, a sound from the bell tinkled and a scratchy very low women's voice came on. "Hello, this is Ms. Wainscott with the Baltimore telephone company, what exchange please?"

"Ahh, I don't have the number could you look it up?"

"What exchange? huh? What neighborhood or is it in center city?"

"Oh, Roland Park?"

"Fine, now name of family resident, please?" I froze thinking was this really all happening?

"Could you see if a Mr. Taybeck, a Percy or Paul or Phillip Taybeck is listed?"

"Hold on." A couple minutes went by, I could hear papers rustling about on the other end then, "Mr. Percival Taybeck on University Blvd. of Bradley Engineering and Survey, Co.?" Yes, that's it. "I'll connect you."

Another young woman was heard on the line named Elizabeth, who said she would get Mr. Taybeck. A high pitched almost boyish male's voice then came on after about five minutes.

From my memorized script rehearsed the night before with a cellar rat and the spider he was eating as an audience in front of my stage of wooden crates, I began. Introducing myself, real name, he wouldn't know me from almost a century yet to come. Told him I was at the Engineer's Club, visiting down from Fall River, Massachusetts and having a cordial time when the discussion came up of a mill up there being relocated on land that you were designing a revolutionary cofferdam for that would drain the marshy site at minimal costs and time. And use the continuous runoff from the now wet stream fed subprime land to provide an auxiliary source of power to the mill in the form of water driven electrical turbines. That's all anyone was talking about all evening. (If this jerk was anything like his great grandson would be, I would hook him with his ego.)

I explained I had just visited the world renown Mr. Abel Wolman at Johns Hopkins and we had discussed whether the system could be designed to incorporate transmission of potable water as well.

The 19th century old great grandfather of that 20th century son-of-a-bitch that crapped on my mom, fell for it hook, line and sinker. A most apropos water metaphor, if I say so myself.

The a**hole was just like his grandson, the apple doesn't fall far from the tree.

I walked the distance, wanted to see more of old Baltimore anyway. No one was in the large house, but it was furnished immaculately, overly cluttered even, not with cheap furniture and junk though. Looked like something from before the civil war, then only fifty years earlier- old fashioned even then. Tacky by today's standards. Percy himself greeted me and I almost cried out, he was a dead ringer for that coward that John had knocked two teeth out of back in the 3rd stall of state highway's sixth floor men's room, except much fatter and with white hair. Turns out I was wrong about the white hair, Percy had taken to donning powdered wigs like English barristers, why? Because he was a nutty Taybeck, of course.

He was a good host though. "First lunch before anything," he said. Between us we polished off about twenty of these tiny sandwiches (I being really hungry and he being really fat) with funny looking bread, called lady somethings with some king of flaky fish and then we had tea, then went to his study.

I wanted to dislike this man, hate him even, but I couldn't. He was generous, smart, funny whistled all the while, and did it very well. although the same blasted two songs, *Beautiful Dreamer* and *Camp Town Races*. After I told him many more lies about myself, it was down to business.

In school, I specialized in hydraulics, so I had a full century more of accrued knowledge about the dynamics of water channeling and retainment than he had since he had been to school. He thought I was a friggin' genius from on high as I reviewed his design with a promise not to divulge any of it as his submitted patent request was still pending approval in Washington. His design may have worked in a more stable foundation environment, as it was to sit on grade with filled ballast tanks as anchors and not be driven pile sheathing. However, the muck that was detailed on his borings for that site wouldn't support a picnic basket evenly to provide a level grade and therefore a seal. He got his idea to set everything just on grade from when they, out of necessity of avoiding more men dying in the caisson from the bends when building the Brooklyn Bridge, just placed the one pier on top of the existing sand grade instead of excavating down to bed rock.

But that was an antediluvian sand that hadn't moved for eons, not Georgian Swamp Muck.

The only 'revolutionary' aspect to his design would be the revolution it made as it sank and turned over bringing the attached sections that happened to be on stable footing down by lateral force. His proposal to counter with spread footers was foolhardy as the load from the cofferdam was lateral sideways from the force of the water being retained against it, not a vertical load that would cause the spread footer to work by using the downward compression of the footer base against the muck's resistance. In short, spread footers or his gloried cheap version of them- the ballast tanks, were not called for nor would they work. I was in the unique position to know the system, as he designed it originally would fail theoretically and historically. I thought to myself, so this is why his 'revolutionary design' failed again and again, bankrupting him. His fault was not so much stupidity, although he seemed dull, bottom of the class material, it was his ego, his want to patent the system and keep it secret that did him in, not allowing anyone else to see it, to bring in another set of eyes as it were.

Well, as fate would now have it, I provided that missing set of 'other' eyes, and those eyes came back from eighty years hence.

We were kindred spirits in how we worked. It was eight o'clock in the evening, when we both looked up from the design plans, hearing his family returning. We both had been in a trance since he yielded and gave me the green light to review his design and suggest changes. This of course, incorporated a tutelage by me on modern, my modern not his, knowledge of hydraulic management. To be fair, his genuine thirst for knowledge, curiosity was ten times greater than his ego, which had caused him to go solo in his quest for fame and fortune, up to this point. He admitted that 'his' system would now work finally only after my input and redesign, where it would not have before. Things got quiet between us again while he then went to his roll top desk and wrote out a note, a long note, in a crude handwritten fashion, silent and abruptly leaving me in the dark, both figuratively and literally, just sitting there for the twenty minutes or so as he feverishly composed.

I was again dumbfounded, not this time by his friendliness and genuine nature unlike his crap descendant I knew, but now by his generosity and deep sense of fair play. The note, stated that if his design was patented and shown to work as designed, that I and my descendants, were entitled to 2.5% royalties to any revenue generated and paid for use of the system by any, and all, other entities other than his company/firm. The just completed handwritten document of his continued on to state that this was in exchange for my consultant expertise on material facets of his design that materially improved upon the design making it more effective and durable. We shook hands, had a wonderful dinner, where I met the Great-grandfather of the future toothless Taybeck, then I departed, declining his offer to have his carriage take me home to my cellar mat on the floor basement rat hole of a home, for obvious reasons. If it all worked as I had planned, now that cofferdam of his will serve its purpose the first time out, the mill will be relocated in the deep south on swamp property now converted to something very valuable and he will not lose his fortune, thereby causing his creep of a great grandson to have to get a job someday in the future with the State of Maryland and be in a position to torment my mother. I could not care any less about what history I might have changed in doing so, and who knows maybe all of this was supposed to even happened in a backward looping, midstream corrective action to man's history. And maybe someday, his promissory note may yield a nice income for me, especially if I must now live all the rest of my days in this time and cannot get back to mine; something I kept fighting not to think about. Losing my family, my friends, my mother and Ruth, a.k.a Red, forever, all at the same time was wholly unbearable. Most importantly though, if my help here and now, meaning back then and there now, let Percy retain the family fortune, then his weasel, women hating off spring would never cross my bow.

Chapter Six
Out and About

Monday mornings are tough wherever and whenever you happen to be. My cell phone alarm went off at 4:15, vibrate only, only after setting the time manually as no signal could be found. I wanted to sneak out of the house through the basement back door before daylight and before the staff of Monumental Engineering filled the office upstairs. With that many eyes and ears just upstairs, the chances that my presence would have become known downstairs were pretty good. Best vacate the premises until late tonight.

The contents of my pockets were a few rubber bands, the ever-present pocket lint, my keys, my flip cell phone, and $26.32 in American 21st century cash, not in 1909 cash. Although a nice sum to get me by for a few days at the going early 20th century rate, it was all useless, and would not pass because of the dates, design and different look. Everything back in my pockets. except my cell phone.

One of those 'divine solutions' coming from the outside universe at large or directly from my coach brother, Tom, now in the Great Beyond, just then popped in my head.

I took the phone's battery out and hid it by wedging it in the seam of that great round coal furnace base and the stone floor and put the rest of the phone in my pocket and made my exit out into the dewy early morning gray before the yellow sunshine cast down on that summer day in 1909 Baltimore. The basement outer sloped doors had knot holes in them that made surveying the back yard easy, although it was still not bright enough outside to see everything. I raised one of the heavy wood doors as I went up the few steps and out I was. The grass was high and wet from dew and the rain yesterday. Remembering the lay of the land from memory I was in the alley in short order with no other telltale signs of my escape than a dog barking close by somewhere behind me. I headed toward the glow of the gas light out front on the street, cornered the alley, around the end of the row of houses, and I was now just another respectable 1909 citizen on my way to work, although my attire made me look like a circus acrobat in comparison to my fellow denizens of the day. A short sleeve collarless T-shirt emblazoned with the dazzling, gaudy colorful outline of the African continent on it; skintight, fitting jeans, and Adidas trainers that only loosely resembled sailor canvas, deck shoes of the day. I stopped and turned my T-shirt inside out, so it showed only white, hopefully helping the situation.

My plans required me to get to the center of Baltimore around the harbor, so I had to find a street name that was familiar and go from there. Other than stumbling over a lamp lighter's unattended ladder and running from a stray dog, first charging the skinny stray hound yelling "go home" three separate times, making me feel lousy because I love dogs more than my kind, I arrived at the harbor's water edge about half an hour after dawn.

The smell was overpowering and nauseating. From school, I knew about the 19th century infrastructure, or lack thereof, that the Jones Falls was used as an open sewer, draining privies by the thousands and the many textile mills from Hamden, a northern Baltimore Mill town, but now it wasn't just academic any longer. The dead fish smell and raw sewage in the warming, June heat almost made me throw up. My fellow pedestrians seemed not to notice the slightest bit though. I quickly backed from the water's edge and headed up Charles Street, the only real main thoroughfare then to go north and south through the city. The sidewalks and street were bustling to the brim even this early in the morning. Many more people walking than I ever saw in my day, which remained to be. I figured this was because most folks now (or I mean then) lived within walking distance of their employment. The traffic, as it were, (horseback riders, horse drawn wagons, horse drawn buggies, bicycles and a few vintage (no, on second thought, current, brand-new cars or horseless carriages and they did resemble carriages without horses more than any modern-day enclosed automobile) in the street was all backed up in grid lock. No horns, but a lot of swearing. Not just a "God Darn", or "Hells Bells" like we were led to believe the pious of that era limited themselves to by the FCC censored Movies, but, "Jesus Christ", "for Christ's sake", "Shit" and I swear I heard the 'F' bomb itself being dropped a few times.

Just by chance, I found the jewelry store that I had always saw on my lunchtime walks when I lived four score years in the future. The only sign it had though, whatsoever, was perpendicular to the street and hanging from a pole coming out from the buildings front wall between the first and second stories, none along the front of the shop's large front window that would identify it to people passing by right out front up against the building, so I had to guess as to its current location from memory or walk far down the street and look back. On my regular twenty first century walks, I always saw the sign in the window, that now had no such information written on it, touting that the firm had been in business for 110 years. It was seared in my memory from repetition of seeing it so many times, and now I could verify that their claim was true, at least for eighty years of the claimed period anyway. I was glad to get off the sidewalk as the ambient body odor of all those people, even in the early morning, was overwhelming. I was no daisy, but God, couldn't they smell each other?

I introduced myself to the original, I guessed Mr. Berman of Berman's Jewelers and he looked at me as if I had two heads. I had a habit of waiting too long to get my hair cut, and now it was problematic in that I had a red afro thanks to the Baltimore heat and humidity of Baltimore in June. Also, the fact I looked like I was someone who forgot to put on his outer garments this morning didn't help at all, of course.

As per my perfect plan, I dove into robust, overly animated conversation using the cheesy Irish accent that I had stolen from the TV 'Lucky Charms' cereal commercials, you know the little Leprechaun always looking for his lucky charms.

Before Mr. Berman could even make sounds come out of his now gaping mouth, I bombarded him with my presence. "Mr. Berman, I am the first mate off the prettiest and fastest oceangoing modern steam freighter afloat, the Queen of the Emerald Isle, now berthed snugly in your beautiful harbor." Without even stopping a second to take a breath I continued. "Owing to some unforeseen difficulties that caused our ship's paymaster to incur a delay paying us until this Friday, I am here to offer you the opportunity of a lifetime to get a rare Chinese treasure I got when there last year, for quite a deal." As I spewed all this manure out in a cheesy, Irish brogue, I, for the first time realized how desperate I was. With this, I plopped my flip phone on the glass countertop in front of the still wide mouth gaping jeweler. Nothing yet said by him, he pulled up a stool and took out his jewelry eyepiece from his vest pocket and set in studying it. A string of intelligible hmms ensued, nothing was said. As I too being a human and a subject to human nature, I too as well became equally transfixed and enthralled with my phone. Our heads were only inches apart in joint study when he startled me by bluntly asking, "What is it?"

As I had overly rehearsed all last night, I said it was both a Chinese locket and a hand agility exercise device that the old timers use there to keep rheumatism at bay and out of their hands. Most are plain, but this one was owned by a big wig's wife, so it is eye catching. Quite fetching really… (I threw in 'fetching' to add credence to my claimed Irish sailor origin). It's called a quai sun. I knew I had him hook, line and sinker, just like I did to Great Granddaddy Taybeck, when he asked, "How does the new cofferdam work?"

"May I?" taking the phone out of his hand, I flipped it open which surprised him as he didn't expect it. On one side there was a shiny black rectangle of glass and on the other, buttons marked zero to nine with a few extra buttons with strange markings. I explained to my new my prospective trading partner that just like our women brush their hair hundreds of strokes a night go get it to shine, the old folks in China regularly count down with these from a very high number, say 250 down to 0 by pressing the buttons repeatedly and this helps ward off the onset of arthritis settling in the hands and fingers. "These quai suns are all the rage in China and really work. Old people there have hands that look just like their grandkids." Boy, was I laying it on thick. There was this old man who played the piano for a living at the moving picture houses over there, he was 98, and he swore it allowed him to keep playing, with no pain, whatsoever, and thereby support his whole family of 82 descendants who were poor as church mice. I was risking burying Mr. Berman in BS, but I had to keep him from thinking too much. The jeweler's glass went back in his eye and for a good ten minutes we both studied the quai sun, tête-à-tête, until once again he startled me by asking what are the small, square, things marked with those strange symbols for and what is the dark glass for. I admitted he got me on the small square things, but they were all called "push buttons" in Chinese, it was a Chinese thing I never found out about those symbols, but as for the glass, I told him the glass is where you place your sweetheart's picture, like in American lockets, the same, exact thing. Oh, yeah, those 'push buttons' marked with English numbers and Chinese symbols are where they push in to exercise their fingers, they come back out all by themselves ready for the operator to use his finger muscles to have to push it in again.

Strengthens the muscles don't you see. Back to more study, while I went to sit down. He then grabbed a big book and kept thumbing through it. He asks what type of metal it was, and I said I think part rare platinum or something like that.

Finally, he stood up and handed me back my cell phone. And started, "Young man, I have been around, but I was young too and had lean times as well. I haven't traveled out of our country, but I do read volumes of everything. I have never heard of these, what do you call them?"

I quickly interjected, "Quai suns, Sir."

"Well, I never heard tell of such, but it is pretty and could be sold to be used as you say. I don't know who made it, but it is precision work, no doubt. I might be being led down the primrose path here by you, but if so, at least it was a good, entertaining tale."

I could feel my face turning red here and feeling red hot. "I'll give you 45 dollars cash for it right now. I countered with $60 and throw in a silver-plated money clip and its yours." He offered $50 and he would even personalize the clip with engraving. We shook hands. I picked out the money clip and wrote the sentiment down that I wanted engraved and asked how long it would take as I wasn't really sure how long I would be here before we sailed out again. Counting out the money, he said that the work would be done by noon that very day. We shook hands again and he asked me to sign a receipt for the cash and transfer of the 1989 cell phone/1909 quai sun and gave me a claim check to pick up the money clip later from his assistant as he would be leaving half day.

Now I was a respectable 'man of means 'although people still stared thinking I was in my PJs or an escaped acrobat from a circus.

First things first, breakfast, breakfast and more breakfast. Where though, no self-respecting eateries would let me in the way I was dressed, and it was still early in the morning. No McDonald's or Burger Kings as most folks here and now, I mean there and then as I write this, ate their breakfast at home. Another stroke of genius from on high and elsewhere. A very good friend of mine and coworker, Leslie, was always after me to go the famous 'Women's Exchange' that had been around for 120 years as of then, but I kept putting it off as it sounded like a lady's foo-foo tearoom kind of deal. Yet one more flash of genius from on high or maybe from more southern climes, I never really know. Unfortunately, it had closed in my time, open one day and shuttered the next, before I ever got there due to procrastination and my rampant insecure masculinity. It was somewhere nearby on Charles Street and as I crossed the street from Berman's shop, I ran right into it. So, I would get there after all, when it was a lot newer than 120 years old. If ever I get back to my office, I will let Leslie know I did get to try it out, before it closed…way before it closed.

To be honest, it sounded quite appealing at this point in my unknown journey, as I was in need of some motherly love, home cooking, about now as I really started missing the folks, Ruth, a.k.a Red, my mom, my co-workers, my pets and the rest of my world back home, and although I kept pushing the thought out of my mind, I really don't know how I got here and if the effect or phenomena will ever reverse or fade away so I can return someday.

When seated, I gave my now pat explanation that I was a newly arrived merchant mariner/sailor, ergo my odd clothes. My waitress, a small woman with jet black dyed hair named Polly was a hoot from the start. Although she never laid eyes on me ever before, I fast became her trusted confidant as to her analysis of her life, friends, the boss and other waitresses in addition to some sketchy looking patrons, besides me. I asked, "What's good?" and she retorted quickly and very loudly,

"Everywhere else," and laughed out loud. I'll trust your choice, Polly. In a matter of minutes, I had a platter full of eggs, ham, sausage, potatoes and some yellow runny stuff as well as Polly's company as she sat herself down during 'her break.' The lady in charge with a permanent grimace kept passing by, so I again spewed a lie and let it be known that Polly was my aunt, Aunt Polly (I tittered to myself, Tom Sawyer also had an Aunt Polly, so I was now in very good company), and asked if it would be ok if we caught up a bit? Mrs. Krumshell, her name, honest to God, consented, more like relented, with a sharp, curt nod and turned away. What a sweetheart.

Poly had been married twice and while married, lived comfortably, but neither of her husband's left much; however, she didn't wallow in self-pity, but got up and went to work right off. She said I looked terrible and smelled worse than most of her customers. So much for customer service. I liked her though. She let me know of a Public Bath on Washington Boulevard near Pig Town in southwest Baltimore that did laundry too. We sat there for almost an hour and Mrs. Krumshell was making tight, repetitive circles all the while, (like a plane in a holding pattern to land of which, of course she knew nothing of), even though the place was empty. It was about 11 a.m. I guessed. my bill was $2.25 and I gave Polly a $1.00 tip. Maybe tipping wasn't around then, or was only around 10 %, as Polly looked like it was her birthday. "That's what we do where I am from, my lady," and gave her a hug. I left Mrs. Krumshell the 75 cents in change and thanked her for allowing our reunion. She then actually broke into a smile. I swear her face cracked as she did though.

I still had two hours to kill before my money clip would be ready, so I visited a bookstore nearby the Washington Monument only a few blocks away, they actually had a first edition of Mark Twain's *Innocents Abroad*, but wanted $18 dollars for it. The word was out as that he was about to come and stay at the Belvedere not a block away as young master Solomon had already let me know about and everything Twain was marked up to coincide with the Twain Fever that was currently thick as thieves in the summer, sultry, rather smelly air of Baltimore of long ago.

I left the basement book shop and climbed up the outside stairs to the sidewalk and then walked over to Baltimore's Washington Monument and climbed the monument's some hundred or so shallow marble white steps to look out over the then Baltimore skyline. I almost blacked out at the top, my stomach was grabbing all the blood to digest Polly's set out feast, and my legs and lungs were in a pitched battle for that same blood. To the south looking down Charles Street, I could see masts and chimneys protruding up on the ships in the harbor but not the ships themselves, and Federal Hill with little black dots that I knew were the same exact ornamental only, nonfunctioning cannon dispersed here and there around the hill's summit that would exist still in my time. Then turning north, with it being so close it loomed over me, was the new Belvedere Hotel all new, shiney,16 stories high, electrified and with all inside plumbing, with a great, cathedral like ceiling three story high ball room on top. My family claimed a personal connection in that my maternal grandparents had, or more correctly would, someday, in but a few short years from that day, meet there for the first time during a ballroom dance. Not that either were rich mind you, friends of friends got them both in. After staring over and fully taking in the early twentieth century Baltimore that lay before me, in full 3D, rich natural color with panoramic vision I was stupefied. Mostly, I was pleasantly taken back by all the vibrant color. Like many of my contemporary Baby Boomers, I had grown to illogically believed everything before the 1960's only existed back then in black and white as all the photographs I ever saw, 'told' me so. To the left of the several schooners masts and steam ship chimneys in the harbor, you could clearly see the famous old familiar Shot Tower. Some 100 feet high, narrow circular brick structure where they made round 'shot' before bullets came along, by dropping molten lead from the top and by the time it plummeted down into the inside water basin below, gravity did its job to 'round' it into balls for firing at bears, the Red Coats and the very recent rightful owners of the land there abouts who might have stubbornly hung around.

While I wasn't very versed on each, and every cathedral and church spire that poked above the mass of low-lying houses, I was well surprised of how many numbers there really were, now that I could clearly see all of their respective steeples and spires that you didn't know were there in my time due to being crowded out of view and lost in a sea of towering buildings.

Given that Baltimore was then predominately Catholic, and there was no suburban sprawl yet to disperse everyone out of the city, these churches were always busy. I saw crowds going to daily Mass down below me on a midweek day much different then home where the places of worship were just for Sunday business only. Baltimore then had many houses of worship of the Protestants and Saturday Sabbath for the substantial Jewish population in town at of the turn into the 20th century, but from my current perch I couldn't see any of them though. I leaned against the blazing white in the sun marble parapet, same as the steps, atop the Washington Monument, trying to catch my breath from the many step climb and not barf out Polly's most ample breakfast. Not alone though, I tried to ignore the nosey guy with a basket full of kittens up there with me, (maybe he was a type I never heard of, a door to door kitten salesman, or maybe it was his intent to chuck them over the side after I left our mutual scenic perch, thereby forgoing the nasty, drowning the litters in a burlap bag that was an accepted practice for animal population control back then all the way up to the time I was a boy in the late 1960's) who just kept staring at me from behind. Busy attempting to blank out his existence by feigning a deep study of the skyline I had ample time to think about the differences between what was then right before my eyes and the world of a few days ago that existed in this same spot. It occurred to me that something, two things actually, were conspicuously absent in this world when looking up in the deep, azure blue summer morning sky.

One, the quarter of a mile high, Baltimore Candle Opera Tower (so called for its three separate major antenna arrangement protruding up from a platform sitting tip top of the support tower beneath, making it look like a Candle Opera) and it's ugly, more modern, single, practical second tower sister sitting adjacent, both being used to broadcast TV and other signals over the entire metropolitan area. These towers could be seen from the suburbs and their sight, always a comforting reassurance, especially after, returning home from multi day absences from our 'Charm(ed) City.'

The second thing I observed as no longer present when scanning the heavens, was the ever present din from of jet passenger airliners, going in and coming from our airport only about 15 miles away to the south and the sound of the Medivac helicopters (taking the trauma victims, including the harvest of night before drive-by drug turf shooting victims to the University of Maryland or Johns Hopkins Hospital's Shock Trauma Units to be miraculously saved at great costs to the taxpayers and patched up to do it all over again until they finally got themselves killed and then buried, again at great expense to the taxpayers). Also, this absence of noise included no city police choppers, 'ghetto birds,' as they have been so euphemistically tagged by the not the so positive, deluded ever-cheery inhabitants, the non-yuppie, non-urban pioneer set. Without the air traffic cacophony, the quiet was deafening, I could hear every little conversation wafting up from the ground, and when there was no sound from the church crowds filling my ears, the nearby kittens mewing in that old freak's basket took over.

If he chucked any of those baby cats over, his sorry ass was going over next. We never exchanged a word up there, early in the morning as my imagination had let my degree of distaste and hate for him multiply by each passing second, so that now I thoroughly abhorred his intrusion into my peace so much so that I was ready to throw him over, just for the fun of it, taking the kittens for my own. It was apparent that the absence of the maximum allowed daily prescription of Prozac for an adult, that I regularly took like clockwork, (that did not make the trip with me), was starting to show in my behavior.

It had now become a waiting game now between the cat seller and I who would capitulate and leave first. I had oodles of time to kill as the Women's Industrial Exchange restaurant did not re-open for late lunch and dinner service for some time yet and I had no job to go to. He did leave eventually, muttering some biblical passage the whole way down the monument that I am sure was meant to damn me and my 'clownish clothes', that's all I could discern clearly out of his babblings during his descent down, into Hell's everlasting damnation I hoped. Good, I further hoped the kittens were all rabid and he got rabies in short order and died wearing a beard of foamy spit bubbles.

I heard a tower clock somewhere strike noon. Down all those marble, far too shallow steps, (needed for the short people back then I figured, but which played hell with you if you were six foot two), to see Mr. Berman's assistant.

We looked as if we were twins, he and I, although he a bit thinner, better dressed and his hair slicked down with something oily. Mr. Hagerty, his name, a weird derivative of the Irish "Hegarty" that made me think he was a Hag or borne from one right from the outset, gave me the clip to inspect and waited. The engraving was just what I wanted and done in a far classier style than I knew to have even asked for. I thanked him, and then he leaned into me and asked about the quai sun, if I could get any more? I promised next time we came to Baltimore after my next visit in China, I'd bring him one. He just said, "Bully." An imitator of the then president, Teddy Roosevelt, He was showing his hand as a sham.

As I turned to go out the door, I almost impaled myself on the free-standing coat rack, that I had not noticed there this morning. Maybe, someone had just placed it there or maybe the red, white and blue ribboned circular straw hat had been added since morning and it made the coat stand more obvious. I only knew one other person who wore that type of hat, my great uncle John and he called it a Campaign hat, thinking that meant political campaign, but he was wrong as a 'campaign hat' was for a military campaign (none of us in my family could ever claim to be the sharpest tacks in the box). It was in fact a skimmer hat. As I said already, my great uncle John, John Baynard, wore one up to, and even in the Nursing Home when only we, his half-sister Beatrice and I, because I drove her, visited him, until his death at 87. Something clicked in my head, but I chalked it up to hunger or a T.I.A. from my vertical monument jaunt and started out the door. As the door closed it opened up again behind me as I still had my hand on the knob, thereby pulling me back in the shop. The young clerk said, "Sir, if you are able to get, say a dozen of those quai suns, I can give you some 'seed' money to purchase them now, before you leave."

Well if I were going to have to live out my remaining days in the early 20th century, I should start "net-working" even though those folks had no idea what that meant. However, I knew this would go nowhere as the product he wanted did not really exist, wouldn't for some eighty years, and then they would be called cell phones and used to talk over and not exercise your arthritic digits while staring all the while apishly at your sweetheart's likeness pasted crudely on black glass. But what harm could it do to hear him out, listen to his pitch.

Mr. Bayard closed the door, turned the door window placard to 'closed' and drew the blinds, which really worked my imagination to the sinister as most of the bright sunshine was now gone and the shop was almost dark, except for the hundreds of little twinkling lights reflecting light from God knows where, coming off the jewelry in the show case, I guessed. things were getting dark both literally and figuratively.

"If you sign a promissory note today, I can front you the money to buy a dozen of those things right now. How much did you really pay for them, don't worry I won't tell old man Berman? This is our deal." Ahh, no employee loyalty back in the good old days either.

"I paid $33 for that one, so $399 or round off to $400 than to that for my effort add say just 20% overhead and profit, so $480 should do it."

I fully expected him to slump down in his chair, but he jumped up and slid a secret wall panel back, (they sure had a lot of sliding wall panels back then) and started whirling a dial on a safe. I had no intention to go this far, I was just playing cat and mouse with him. There were five crisp one hundred dollar bills placed on my lap, reminding me when that contractor tried to bribe in back at my job in the future. As he set in to writing, I assume the promissory note I was to sign, I asked if Mr. Berman needed to okay the cash release. "That old guy, he won't miss it for months, he's a bit touched in the head if you know what I mean. Crackers."

Oh my God, only one other person I ever knew ever used that phrase verbatim and in that tone of voice and in that manner. I was hyperventilating. All that genealogy hogwash my brother did now was sinking in, the years were right…he would be about 25, the place even that damn silly skimmer hat with the patriotic red, white, and blue ribbon. This cutthroat, backstabbing fool was none other than my own flesh and blood, my Great Uncle Mr. John Baynard himself. The coup de gras give away was when this weasel was about to steal from his boss to feather his own nest along with a stranger that he didn't even know. From what I remember hearing from the family about him, he was a real bastard; three wives, placed two of his kids in orphanages, got so drunk once, his other little boy drowned in front of him. So here was my family tree. Although, he looked just like me now, however, back in the nursing home when he was in his mid-eighties and I visited him as I felt sorry for him that the rest of the family had all but disowned him, he was a frail, white haired man, eliciting sympathy from me and those all around him. He was a charmer, wheeling up and down the nursing home in his patriotic skimmer hat, enjoying privileges no other residents had, simply because, as I know now, he was a sinister, sociopath. I couldn't hate him then at his end in the nursing home, but he sure turned my stomach now, standing there in front of me in flesh and blood, a mirror image of myself. "It wouldn't be fair for you to have to lay out all that money up front and I am really not sure, when we'll go back to China, at least that part where I bought the quai sun. I tell you what, rewrite the promissory note that you agree to buy all twelve units when I deliver, at my purchase price plus the 20 % overhead and profit, and when I do get them, I will come back here, no matter where on the east coast we berth, and deliver them." He ripped up the old note he had just scrawled out hastily and gave me a signed note that referenced the quai sun by name. We shook hands, it felt like clapping with an eel, and I got out of there as fast as the wind. It is true, you can pick your friends, but not your ancestors though. What a friggin' bottom feeding turd.

I put the note safe in my pocket that if ever this spell or warp in time dissipates and I return, I am going to dig up my great uncle's signature on something in his nursing home era and compare for sure. If I ever return here again afterward, then I will give this note to Mr. Berman someday so he can fire that piece of scum and if he died from starvation. penniless, early, say 60 years early, then good. And if his dying early screwed up the future world, causing me to vaporize into vast nothingness, so be it, also okay, because as I've said in here before, I am a vindictive, vengeful bastard, and first things first. Walking down the street about 20 minutes later I realized that no one ever learned of his deceit, as I was still walking and didn't disappear, so maybe that means I do get back to my time. Now I was happy again and forgot about my slug relative. Wonder when and why this charlatan changed his name from Hagerty to Baynard? If ever I get back, I'll ask my brother Michael to research it.

Now off to get cleaned up and smelling like a rose again. As I was relatively rich now, I took a streetcar out to Pig Town and the public bath. The place reminded me in every respect as my gym's sauna, except, much darker inside and no trunks and it wasn't co-ed. There were men from 70 to boys of five, and during a workday.

I really think they were more using the place as a pool, to get away from the June heat and high humidity outside, than a bath. My laundry was washed and dry and wrapped in brown paper when I was leaving about 4 p.m. I noticed though something odd, that there was a note pinned to the elastic band on my briefs containing only a sole character '?' How they got them dry and starched, in that two-hour period, I'll never know. Ever wear a starched T-shirt and briefs? It's a new experience I can tell you, my nipples and other unmentionable things were raw for two days.

On public transportation out on the Catonsville trolley, though this one was pulled by horse even though it had the electric transmission pole on top, it just wasn't working I guess and they reverted back to the old tried and true 'Bessie' who had just recently been retired to pasture, and gladly not the glue factory. I wonder if she was mad or glad about it, I mean going back to productive service. It did mean oats and hay for dinner and not only grass. The seats had straw in the cushions that made a crunching sound whenever someone sat down. I arrived at my destination about 5:00, dinner time. I've always seemed to arrive at friend's houses at dinner time, what a leech.

I was directed to the administration office at the St. Mary's Industrial School by a nun wearing an apron over her black robes. It was dinner time and I guess they had bare bones staff. And great, the administrator turned out to be a priest, not a layman administrator. Now after I told this whopper of a lie that I was planning to tell and to a priest, I was going to hell, absolutely. I explained to Father that I was an Irish merchant marine off the 'Emerald Isle' berthed in Baltimore, that was undergoing repairs for a month (this and what follows was such a last minute, spontaneous improvement on my fictitious life that even I was beginning to believe it, it was getting so rich and full of detail) and to help make ends meet, to send money back to my widowed, destitute mother in Dublin, I took on this very temporary courier job in Baltimore. My assignment was to personally deliver this package that I held today, before night fall, and get the receipt signed by the party. Father John or Thomas, I don't remember now, took the package and kind of smirked and sighed when looking down at the name. He let me know that the recipient was a student who was at dinner at that very moment in the cafeteria and if I could wait a little, he would go and get him.

While I waited, I looked out the window. A lot of streets and roads in the then 1909 suburbs of Baltimore were narrower than 2009, when they were in the county proper, and houses that were right on the sidewalks back in my home time now had expansive front lawns. The price of progress, road widening had gobbled up their lawns leaving the houses practically in the road. And a chorus of sounds of slowing turning blades as men were busy, all in white, high buttoned up shirts, soaked with sweat, cutting their lawns with man powered push mowers.

When the priest came back, the young man in tow was not who I expected. He had almost blond, tight curly hair, bleached by the summer sun maybe, and as lean as a whippet. A small framed 14-year-old, not like his pictures, as a grown man. The priest told him that I was a messenger and had a package for him and that he had to legally sign. Immediately the boy started to eagerly sign the receipt with a big smile on his face, like he was quite familiar with the procedure. The Father slowed him down and said it was good practice to inspect the contents first, before receiving any package by messenger. It really wasn't I believe, even though I wasn't a real member of the package delivery profession, I knew that the Father was fibbing just so as to see the contents as well. Well, that made two bona fide liars in that room, the Father and me, and maybe even three, giving that young George was a boy in this glorified reform school after all. After opening the package, the kid grabbed the five one-dollar bills retained by the silver clad money clip, but let the clip fall back into the now crumpled brown wrapping paper. Father William or Peter, Tom or Fred, I can't remember now, retrieved the clip and saw the inscription and told the boy to sit down. He read it as if reading from the pulpit. "To George Ruth, Jr., keep up the good work as a baseballer. A patron of the sport, JAM."

The priest folded the money and showed George how it was to be placed in the money clip. Saying it would be kept safe for him until he graduated. Looking at me, he dismissed me as my job was done, and then had the kid sign the receipt to which Father signed on as guardian and witness. I got up to leave, got to the door when I heard, "Thanks, Mister." I walked backed in the room tousling the boy's curly hair and said, "Mark my words, George, you will be great and loved by many." Father Sam or Eric or Steven looked at me as if I were a lunatic as I made the hastiest of exits.

On my way back from my coup to see Babe Ruth, I was quite proud of myself. Patting myself on my back for the planning and execution and having his autograph now on the receipt to boot, even though it didn't say Babe, but George H. Ruth, Jr. If I ever get back to my job, my life in my original time, I can now take an early retirement state retirement at twenty years and live off the proceeds of the signed receipt along with my reduced early pension. That wasn't my entire intent though to see him, to make money, it was the same as those who climb Mr. Everest, because it, in this case, he, was there.

Walking down Washington Boulevard, people started looking, staring and gawking at me, sometimes one of these actions alone, others doing all three whether it be one person or three or more. Out here, now in the suburbs, a tall Irish man wearing funny clothes and a red afro as caused by the soupy, humid Baltimore air, was not a daily occurrence. Not to mention my skin tight jeans, finely tailored, strapless overalls by the current standards, and starched rigid T-shirt with the African continent on it that even though inside out, revealed the underneath outline when the T-shirt was sweat drenched – (oh how I missed air conditioning). I did notice most of my gawkers were women and that inflated my ego to no end.

Thank God Baltimore is a midsize to small town, and even smaller then, I mean now, when it comes to relying on Shank's mare for transportation. Halfway back to the city's center was my next point of interest.

The Historic Mount Clare Mansion, oldest colonial mansion in the country, was historic even now, I mean then, that is to really say now in 1909.

It contained a mystery that we at the Baltimore City Department of Transportation-2009 version had uncovered when performing peripheral improvements to this grand dame of a structure and grounds as a tack on to the work we were doing on the nearby Interstate Highway I-95 that shaved the estates grounds. While performing test on the soil, we penetrated an unknown, old underground tank that contained an also unknown liquid from back then. Our first thoughts were that it was lamp kerosene gone bad over centuries, but when all manner of tests didn't back our theory up, our Snap Design Team at the Maryland State Highway Administration, (local office anyway as this was our baby and we didn't share potential career advancing work, all of us being petty and attention craved; pretty much the essence of being a bureaucrat) we accepted the challenge to find out what was in the tank and what it was used for, not to protect the public from potential hazard material harm, but more for shits and giggles, as they say, whoever "they" may someday eventually turn out to be.

Now, I had eighty percent of a century jump on my colleagues to figure this out, so we could move our work along if ever I got back, but more importantly so I could win the $218 dollars now in our office pool for the winner of 'Figure out the Muck in the old tank contest'.

The 'Historic Landmark' designation back when and where I was from, meant almost nothing here, just a label. The place was a dump now, not the colonial style gem it would someday be returned back into. Trying to get my bearings in the now, what could only be called a junk yard with a ramshackle house in the center, I made tons of noise along with my inevitable 'f' bombs and associated lesser swearing each time I fell in debris. No park service guards then to worry about. Sitting there holding pressure on a new gash to my shin so I wouldn't bleed out, (OK, maybe a tinge overdramatic) I distinctly heard the sound of electronic tones/music nearby. Thought it might be my cell phone picking up an errant signal from 1989, like seeing that jet fly over the first night back in this time, weak probably only one bar, but then I remembered Mr. Berman had it.

I didn't feel too bad about if I made some money on the flip phone, it was State issued, a prototype that they were using with us as guinea pigs of sort to test the durability of the flip design and varying EMF output depending on local tower availability, to see if we had our brains fried or not- the thinking being that civil servants could risk brain damage and still function in a satisfactory manner until retirement. Just kidding, I had a relative in the business who got me to test the prototype for free usage a full five years before they planned to release it. Anyway, back to the dilapidated mansion of Old Maryland gentry- a close relative to a signer of the Declaration of Independence.

Then a cascading sound of lumber and the prettiest most melodic, 'Oh, Shit.' She was about 28 years old down to 21 if under perfect mood lighting and music with wine. Dark complexion with the kind of dark, silky hair that has that natural sheen on it. Now, I could hear the recorded music tones even louder as the thing she had in her hand flew when she fell, with the earphones, or ear buds as I later found out they were called, both flew out separate ways. It was music.

Lifting the wood off of her, I took more time than really necessary as she was cute, beautiful even, and I kind of wanted to savor the unwrapping. Her name was Lalanya. No blood, no broken bones were reported by her. Before I could begin to find out her story, she starts cross examining me.

Where did I live, across the way in Morrell Park, Pig Town? Why was I dressed that way? Where did I get those Shoes…? "Hey, not to be sexist, but you are the damsel in distress, and I am the gallant rescuing prince."

"Who are you and what the hell are you doing with a Walkman cassette player in 1909?"

I decided no more pretense, this was some f**ked up mess here, that had now killed my libido or at least knocked it back on its heels for a few.

Lalanya, broke up laughing. "Walkman, cassettes, Adidas tennis shoes and Live Aid T-shirt, and that hair, you look like something out of my father's year book."

"Huh?" is all I could manage.

I was 'smitten' in the vernacular of the day by this sexy, alpha dog, of a younger woman. So much for the obvious questions posed by both of us to both of us. "My name's James and how do you know about all this stuff and of things yet to be," I barked in a no nonsense, take control way.

"Not yet to be, but already been and gone you mean," she came back with. She said I should lay off trying to be Victorian poetic as it didn't fit me and came across as me being a big a**hole. Now we were talking the same language. Picking up her high end, Walkman like gadget and weird wireless ear phoney things, I could hear the music playing even louder now. Jesus, it was that old song, *Don't fear the Reaper* by Blue Oyster Cult from when I was a kid. That's it, I did die back in my office, not just passed out and this had been some sick, twisted dream state that my conscious is now in to keep me entertained and busy as my body, who's job of entertaining me it used to do, is now dead and decomposing somewhere. Not bad, I don't remember any pain or even indigestion.

She brought me back to earth though with. Well, I guess you already visited Babe Ruth, huh?

OK, what was this? She went on that most of the time travelers she runs in to who find a way back there by hook or crook, do it just to kiss Babe Ruth's butt. Most of those doing that from her experience were older, flabbier, type men with a stunted boyhood complex and I didn't seem to fit the type. And it might be said that as he was only a kid now, that they might be classified even as pedophiles, just what the Catholic school he is staying at needed more of like ice for Eskimos. She declared that I looked like I care about my health, fitness and other things more than baseball. Boy, she could flirt. I didn't think I was flabby.

So she was on to this time travel thing too. This was some crazy shit to take in, or maybe my disembodied consciousness was on a freak holiday, running on over drive in the afterlife.

Almost every time I come back here on my stint to safeguard this site, I see others, who stand out like sore thumbs parading back down that road back there into the city, proud as peacocks that they got to see that kid. "I didn't only see him, but gave him a gift," I proudly added.

"Well, doesn't the sun just shine out of your ass." Ah, a fellow potty mouth on a beautiful young lady, I was in love.

"This is an iPad that plays MP3's as well as internet direct downloads, not a cassette tape player, Grandpa."

"You are listening to Blue Oyster Cult, Grandma," I sharply retorted.

We spent the rest of the day together in a room she had decked out in the basement of the old Mount Clare mansion that was hidden behind a false wall. There was a refrigerator, real food, and praise be, air conditioning. A small room in the back of this was her office/ living quarters with real plumbing and hot water. Her job was to secure and maintain that tank and its contents, the very same that me and my coworkers were obsessed with back 1989. She wouldn't say what was in there or how it got there, only that the tank was not as old as we thought, not man made and the contents were extremely hazardous and should be avoided until a time when her and her co-workers can figure out how to disarm and safely remove it someday. She knew everything about our efforts of finding it and stupidly poking about it like monkeys poking sticks against a hornet's nest. They, her and her outfit, had even found the weaken area and repaired it where our people, me and my work gang, had tried to just puncture the tank and just drain it away and forget about it. Only if she knew that that puncturing and draining away move was my sole idea and personal contribution to our team's attempted creative, en vogue, thinking outside the box, resolution to the mystery tank and contents. Small world, huh?

While she couldn't, or wouldn't share how she got there and her colleagues came back and forth from her time to safeguard the area, she did share with me, "That there were things not now understandable at work here to any of us, especially given that of all people and of all times, that it was me now brought here, the very one who thus far almost singlehandedly destroyed the tank, releasing its hellish contents." While she didn't bother defining her, "hellish contents" remark, she did remark that I was very apt at f**king things up big time. So, she did know me very well after all. I hoped I could very soon return the favor. I always get relaxed and horny when scared and stressed. My personal varied "Fight or night-night complex."

I thanked her, passing this off as a compliment, all press is good press after all, if you can't be famous, infamy will do as I always say. She did say that she was as dumbfounded as I was why I, of all people, should be brought here and now to learn this secret, but she thought that I could now call the circus off with me and the other monkeys in my office tinkering with things far beyond our comprehension. I promised her that I would if I ever got back, but now she owed me one. Sometimes when things are so surreal, so incomprehensible the best thing to maintain your sanity, is just to go with it, best to sometimes just do nothing, as Winnie the Pooh said. Unlike me, who had no idea how I leaped vaulted back eight full decades, this young lady, only coming back from a generation after my time back home, seemed to have master this feat along with her colleagues on a regular basis, clocking in and out work hours, that were being paid for…this was her job.

No matter how I tried to craftfully get information from her, she was not forthcoming, almost as if she had been trained not to divulge anything. In fact, she had been so trained as she admitted to me under more comfortable circumstances in a far more laidback setting later. The reason being as they were charged with minimal interaction with those in this time, and as like with me, of any other time this made sense as the idea of upsetting the apple cart of history was blinding. To that end, her team, established their monitoring office-station at the now dilapidated vacant old building, where few people ever went. While there, each person served a three-day shift monitoring the tank and its contents and also the area for intrusion. They were allowed to go in town, on their off hours at night only with minimal to no impact or interaction as they had been trained to do…Fraternizing, beyond polite salutations, were not allowed. Use of any substances that may impair their judgement, not allowed either. (Damn, then why even bother going in town, I thought) They had a complete wardrobe of period clothes for both men and women to wear on such outings. This was all so unbelievably surreal.

They had patched into the local phone lines, as limited as they were, running off a locally established party line of the railway station nearby in Morrell Park.

I asked if I had screwed all this up, she paused and said that as I evidently was supposed to be there in that time, that she guessed not irreparably so. "Guessed," oh my God, that was very confidence inspiring. By her refence earlier to the parade of people going to look at young Babe Ruth, there must be more than one way to skip back and forth in time. This was my first real hope that maybe I actually could get back, now things looked and felt a lot better. Just like being on a vacation to an exotic place for only a set prescribed number of days. I though knew of none of this before and just seem to stumble across it, as I have done with most good things in my life.

After whining and cutting a deal with her to share as many details about the tank that I knew, but had never put in any official report, she agreed to let me see what they had so far done with it which consisted of primarily reinforcing the tank with a protective fibrous flexible, but high tensile strength covering with motion and other types of sensors around the property and on and in the tank itself, to fend off my suggested just piercing it in eighty years to come and letting the contents run out.

Some of what they were doing I understood, but much of it I had no idea about. I started to believe she was from further in the future than only one generation ahead of me or I was just too dumb to learn and visualize what was to come, much like Percy Taybeck was when I tried to enlighten him.

She asked about my tale of woe. Why I was here, why I came back. As one professional to another far more beautiful professional I was not going to say I had no idea of anything, other than I wanted to get the goods on some scum that abused my mother, so I said I had come back to investigate the large great Baltimore fire debris fill field adjacent to the Jones Falls in Baltimore near the soon to be built new Penn Station.

"Investigate it for what?" she asked.

"Nothing dangerous in that area, but harmless remnants of building debris." Lalanya had me, they, in their work, knew what was hazardous, what needed to be clean up, and what was a bull shit story, like I was then spewing.

"OK, I am a lowly, put upon too many times, civil servant trying to get the goods on a corrupt contractor and the whole corrupt, political machine controlled local government sponsoring him and his cronies."

"Why, is it so important to you, is the money coming out of your pocket?" she smiled when she said it. I was about to burst, when she said, "No need, I know all about you. To sum it up, you have a chip on your shoulder against authority, and as soon as you see a chink in their armor, you go at it. Not for any noble cause, but for the shear fun of it. It's psychological, a pathological payback syndrome for when you were young and couldn't fight back." Well thanks, I said in a false bravado, as I was collapsing inside as it all hit home, I wish, I ran across you ten years earlier, I would have saved a lot in analysis sessions. All she said is, "Let the chip go, it's about time Mr. Quixote. I will tell you this, that your efforts, although of dubious motivation, will prevail in this matter of yours and another far more important one regarding health and safety, in two crucial separate and distinct additional matters. Whatever the driving cause and force it created, perhaps it was meant to form you and buttress your nature for just such campaigns."

I wanted to yell back a very mature "say's you" to her, but she was right, and she knew how this would work out for me and that in the end, it all would. What a rare gift she had just given me.

When they do allow you to go out on the town, for social purposes is it always by yourself, solo I mean?

Damn, I sound like a fourteen year old asking for a date, Well would it be possible for both you and I both together, to trip the light fantastic in Baltimore tonight, we and the future should then be safe, right? "Well, James, how could I resist such an invitation from a silver tongue devil like you.' I was completely and utterly happy then, more so than I remembered that I ever had been, even with Ruth, a.k.a. RED, and that scared me."

Night fell, she set some kind of laser activated trip alarms at the site and when we got back to her office, she said she was now off-the-clock till 8 a.m. next morning and asked me out for crabs and beer on her company expense account. (Thank God that expense accounts have been around since George Washington was a General and, by all accounts, no pun intended, will be for all time and eternity.) The beer I was up for, the crabs possibly not, remembering what the harbor smelled like that morning.

She called me spineless and then added, "That when in Rome." She went in the rooms behind her office to get ready and when she came back had replaced her tan jump suit type outfit with a period dress and brought me a white, balloon sleeve like shirt, brown, rough material pants and black boots saying they were just a loan for tonight.

The shirt and pants were too big and the boots that were too small. She hooked my suspenders, so I considered the ice to be if not broken, open for melting. What a shallow cad I am. Once we were dressed, it was obvious she was going formal and I informal.

I pointed this out and also finally admitted that crabs were not my thing, even in 1989, but even more so since I saw the Jones Falls and smelled it of late. "Hold that thought," we are going uptown. After rummaging for a half an hour, she found me shoes to replace my boots, the shoes were still too small, and a dinner jacket fit okay and a celluloid high-top collar.

Once we were both dressed, looking like extras from Central Casting, she handed me a modern day, landline type phone receiver and asked me to order a cab to pick us up at the Mount Clare entrance on Washington Blvd. She said that it wouldn't be proper for a lady then to use the phone to order a cab. Guess where we were off to? The ball room of the Belvedere Hotel.

"Will the cab be an automobile or a horse and buggy kind of thing you think?" I asked Lalanya as we started walking down the old weed covered cobble stone drive to Washington Boulevard, her having a lot more trouble with heels, although my too small shoes weren't a picnic either.

"I have no idea, does it matter?"

"No, not really, but I'd like to sit next to the driver to watch him operate such an old car." It came off as a plea, more than just an item of conversation.

"Let's just walk in the grass, or I will twist my ankle, if you sit up front, and leave me in the back by myself, the cab driver might think we are at odds, don't you think."

"Can't we just tell him I am fascinated to distraction with these new automobiles?" It came out as a shrill begging, my voice always goes into the head, a falsetto tenor, when I get real excited.

She smiled, now walking barefoot in the grass holding her evening shoes, "Men take a lot longer to mature from boys than women from girls in any age it seems."

"While everyone back home, settles for automatic transmission and cruise control, my car has a manual stick transmission, I ordered it new that way, they even had to bring it in from two states away. I bet I could easily drive these cars now." Then it occurred to me for the first time in my life that 'car' was short for carriage. I really, really hoped it was an automobile cab and not a horse drawn carriage cab.

We sat on the bench at the corner edge of Morrell Park, where I told the cab company we would be waiting. "Look here JAM, today is your lucky day." She handed me a five-dollar bill and said that if I told the cabby I was an experienced driver already, and offered him the $5, he might just let me drive it some, that is if they sent an automobile and not a horse and carriage. My recently departed mother would be rolling over in her grave back home, as she always told me a lady never pays on a date (that and don't open your mouth and people might not catch on how dumb you really are) and now I was a kept man, so to speak, with Lalanya picking up the tab for eats and the ride. I could get used to being a Gigolo. Beside all that, now I was kind of frightened. Lalanya called me JAM. Only Ruth (a.k.a Red) had ever called me JAM, short for James Allan Morrison, what gives? I point blank asked her how she knew. James everything will work out for you and her, one day it will be common knowledge to many, including your children, about that endearment of hers for you well as your 'RED' for her. I couldn't form a word to respond even. I was in ecstasy.

Honestly at first, I thought it was an errant swan from behind us in the park when I heard the deep, responding honk, honk. It was the hand squeeze horn on the cab, an automobile.

After crossing my heart, a bit juvenile, but it did the trick, the cabbie took the $5.00 dollars and said that I could drive until we got to Pratt Street that ran alongside the harbor – about three miles.

I was all ready to impress him when I jumped in his seat. Ollie, the cabbie's name, yelled, "Not so fast, got to start her up first," and he then jumped out of the automobile, with a tire iron looking thing and disappeared in front of the engine.

After hearing gears turn three times in the engine somewhere, Ollie came up to my door and again yelled, I think he was deaf or just extremely rude.

"Sir, didn't you tell me you have driven many miles before?"

"Yes, Ollie, but only in England, you see I'm a sailor and—"

He stopped me and said, "Don't know about England, but here you have to pull the choke out halfway and fiddle with the throttle while I turn the starter."

"Of yeah, I do recall hearing that Yank, we're a bit behind in all that." I was getting real good at lying, but he didn't seem to appreciate it wiping the unnecessary sweat that I caused from his forehead. After a brief primer on the choke and throttle operation he went around front of the automobile again and on the second try, the engine roared, more like sputtered, to life. Lalanya was laughing hysterically in the back seat.

Ollie came around the front passenger seat, put the starter rod between us in this brass box that had coals in it, heater for winter he said when I asked, took his cabbie hat off that had the badge on it and put it on my head, and after a few jumps and jolts we were off, on Washington Boulevard. In my day (to come) I had driven in England, Ireland? Manhattan and Pittsburgh, all the best challenges, (Pittsburgh the worst hands down, but you didn't hear that from me) and now I was driving in another time. Once you learned to steer clear of the trolley tracks that would grab and redirect your front wheels the ride was much better. It was like being in a parade as the automobile was still a novelty, a kid tried to jump on to the running board on my side, I squeezed the horn ball and he ran back to the sidewalk, but in doing so, the horse of the carriage in front of me got spooked and left a large pile of his type of exhaust which we just rode through like all the other piles, albeit this one a lot more fresh and wet. Just when I was getting the hang of it, I could see the masts over the houses of the ships in the approaching harbor. My face gave me away surely as Ollie then yelled over the loud engine noise, "Young Sir, you can take her right up Charles Street to the door of the Belvedere if you would like. I can tell you know how to drive." (Oh, if he only knew that I average 30,000 miles a year on my cars at home with my 100 mile a day roundtrip commute from Mayberry outside Westminster to Baltimore.) When we pulled up, we thanked Ollie and asked if he could take us back around 11:00.

He said, "of course, as he would be the only driver of an automobile cab at night." He also said, "If ever I was looking for work to call his company and he would vouch for me." A real possibility, I might have to consider, at least short term, if I had stay here awhile or even forever.

When my grandmother and grandfather had met there the three story high ballroom still existed as it did now. By the time I was dating, it had been cut down into separate floors of a restaurant and a bar. I always wanted to see the old ballroom, where the idea of my father's conception may have started, and now I was going there too.

The elevator had an operator and a cage that came across, like in all the old movies.

Before we were seated Lalanya handed me a roll of bills to pay the check as she couldn't then. Lalanya's complexion, that of a woman from India, and mine, a man from paper white Ireland did conflict and stand out a bit, but as she was "exotic" looking, I figure the closed minded of the day, let it pass. Had she been just a tad darker, they wouldn't have let her come in the front door even.

No shop talk, no time leap frogging talk, we just conversed, about what she liked, what I liked, about kids, dogs, India, pleasant grown people talk. Once I had a few drinks, she couldn't and maybe for the same reason, I shouldn't have, though she was there to watch I didn't slip and change history, we got up to move about, it wasn't dancing, at least not on my part, but it sure felt like I was dancing on a cloud the whole evening, a cliche that I always thought to be cheesy until that night. She was perfect.

On the way home, there was no question even to the rest of the night, as I had her company's borrowed clothes on that she had to get them back off of me.

Early next morning, while walking home in my T-shirt again, I cursed fate a bit, as to try to pursue it any further would have been 'complicated' and that's a gross understatement. Some things never change, do they?

In the end though, aside from respecting this young lady's professional commitment, intelligence and appreciating her natural beauty and sense of humor, I had to trust her beyond any doubt, which I did. For you see in 1909, not too many all-night pharmacies were around and even if they were, I don't believe they made those things only needed by guys to hold up their end of the deal. This department was under her sole control then, and as promised it had been addressed, the green light was on. If it hadn't, then you might say we may have literally screwed up the future.

I walked up Washington Blvd at 4 a.m. toward my cellar basement home, dodging stray dogs and fat rats and two separate cops walking their beats, doing that baton swirl thing that you use to see in the movies, as they walked back and forth.

All went well in my total pitch-black entry back into the basement, even the neighbor's dog, named Cleopatra, as I heard her being called, was quiet, aside from her of tail thumping noise as she gobbled down the doggy bag I got her from the Belvedere, and because she had gotten to know me and liked me. One snag though, quite literally, I had forgotten about the odd placement of the upright water hand pump smack dab in the center of the basement stair landing. As I stumbled myself toward my crates and my cushy mat, that warm post injury feeling that only men get when running into objects waist high dead center came on me rather quickly. Later on while still on the bare stone floor, in the fetal position that is required with such injuries, I saw a new canvas bag, more apples and soda crackers and that someone, or some little lady, had put, three daisies in between the crate slats. And wrote. Mr. Morrison, we miss you. Are you still here?

With nothing to do now in the dark and quiet, I just laid there and started to think. At this very moment how many people, long gone in my home time, are very much alive, breathing, hearts beating, busy going about everyday life. Sure, there are the Thomas Edisons, Winston Churchills, and Teddy Roosevelts now about and kicking, however, just as important, Esty and her parents sleep, now healthy and living with only two floors separating us, only to be a dusty wisp of memory in my time. What her grandchildren would give to be in my place. I also thought about whether Esty, Solomon, Percy and Lalanya would even remember me, if I would make any mark on their lives and if it might be better that what was to come later without me, or had I made things a lot worse.

It is good that I didn't let Solomon know that somehow, I came back in time a full eight tenths of a century as eventually it would occur to him that maybe I could do it again, a few years earlier next time and warn his father about the impending tragedy that took his life.

Although mind blowing, this time was just like any other, fundamentally. People woke each morning, spent their days working and spending time with each other, then got tired and went to sleep each night. Teenagers filled with hormones fell in love and started families, the old folks fell into introspective reflection, wrapping it all up before moving on. While back here in 1909, the "stage" that they now trod upon is just as new, vibrant and brightly lit as ours in my home time, contrary to our modern day conceitful and arrogant perception that somehow it was not so, given our misplaced vain sense of sophistication and exceptionalism grounded solely and artificially in technical advancements. I can now attest firsthand that in both of these times, the stage for us all is identical and just so much background to Life; that once crossed, will be left behind to not exist as it is not needed any more as those who played upon it take their leave.

Like a magician, I could temporarily astonish and befuddled these folks with tales of things to come; jet planes that speedily fly 400 people around the world at a time in complete comfort, color television, cell phones, space travel, but their astonishment would be short lived and very soon pass, once they came to the inevitable realization that these really do not connote a better, more, civilized and sophisticated society to come. Having more gadgets, better and easier tools, less work and more free time on one's hands, didn't make us any better. We lived longer they would see thanks to further advancements in medicine, that came about based on work started in their day, but we than just floundered aimlessly too often in this bought "extra time." All these new shiny bells and whistles, distractions as they now have become, that our 21st century claims as their accomplishments alone, were in the works for centuries, with most of the truly revolutionary breakthroughs occurring right about the time I am in now. Given this fact, these improvements of things only can't be worn and shown off as a badge of any real societal advancement by any one particular time and its people, least of all my home time, with its human underpinnings crumbling unceasingly.

More astonishing to these folks, nay, more frightening, would be to tell them that not only one world-wide war would be in the cards just a handful years down the road, horribly killing millions, but it would be then eclipsed in horror misery and wholesale cruelty beyond comprehension in less than a half of a lifetime after. If those who were sleeping sound as I then tried to get to sleep only knew, they too would then be sleepless.

Telling them that the average life span would be almost doubled in the next hundred years would most assuredly cause their mouths to fall agape, but when I go on to let them know that many fill this extra allowed precious time with despicable vices of distractions to 'kill time,' to while away all the new found hours, I am sure they will glad to be born when they were and would pass on the future and extended life given those terms.

In the end, if there really is an afterlife where we all mingle from all ages and times, very soon all the superficial differences from when we lived would melt away, leaving only the fundamental differences of how we chose to live out our days. Whether we cared for each other and shared in the face of our time's trials and adversities, believing our lives were not the end all, or locked up our hearts and closed our minds, fortifying ourselves in the faithless belief that to survive and thrive our assigned days in the mortal coil was all there was and to only make it through it was all that mattered. Before falling off to sleep though, I thanked God my mind left the realm of the profound and returned to TV rerun trivia.

Next day, Tuesday, same thing, out by four-ish in the AM, before dusk. Safely in the back alley not near any house any longer, I reached up along the wooden wall of the barn like structure that Solomon lived in trying to find the cord that little Miss Esty used to get Solomon's attention a day or two before. I couldn't find it in the dark and started cussing, really major league cussing. Just as I finally found the blasted string and was about to pull it to ring the bell, a little nightcap poked out between the doors that opened with a loud "Shhhhh." I wasn't going to say it, of course, but at first it looked like a KKK hood. I think the humor would have been lost on the teen African American young man. Solomon said, "With all due respect," Mr. James, if you keep talking like that using those ugly swear words, you ain't going up when you die, but down to the other place." I apologized and said I will try not to anymore. I also let Solomon know I was sorry for just disappearing like that, but had errands to run. If he could let Esty know this, I sure would appreciate it. Also, let her know I got her flowers and C.AR.E. package, then I corrected that as that organization wouldn't come to be for almost 40 years on. Thank her very much and for the daisies and note on the crates. Owing to you two, this lost soul is a happy man, now content with his lot in this new life. You guys are my best buds. At this, I could see Solomon's head, cocked to the side, questioning what I had just said.

"Never mind, let it go son. Look, tomorrow If you see me talking to your boss in the morning, pretend not to know me and don't worry. Keep a secret? You and I are going to meet Mr. Mark Twain himself, come hell or high water. Sorry, Solomon, I'll try to stop really." He didn't hear my second apology for being a potty mouth, as he had since jumped out of the doors by then and was by my side. Mr.

James, about tomorrow, I already tried to get the day off, even work Sunday to make up for it, but Mr. Simon said no, he couldn't spare me. "Look kid, I promised and have a plan where you and I will not only see him, but travel there in style on one of your horse and wagon rigs. I will hire your services and the wagon to help me move. "Do you have a lot of stuff Mr. James?"

"No, nothing really, but he won't know that. Mr. James, I am afraid I will never see you in heaven, ever," the little man wrapped in a boy's body most matter of factly stated. I laughed and said that he and Esty will help me be better from now on and I will most likely get in as I'd have both him and Esty already there to lobby for me."

At this, Solomon's eyes squinted, "What do you mean?"

I quickly recovered and said that we visit heaven even in our dreams, so they could vouch for me one night in dreams when I die and try to get in way before them. Whew, I must either think better on my feet, or just shut up with all the extraneous musings of mine altogether. I asked Solomon if he could get back in and back to bed and he reminded me he was already up to feed the horses and begin the coals in the blacksmith furnaces. (No child labor laws in 1909, so much for the good ol' days.) I hugged this sweet kid, he didn't see my tears and off I walked around the corner cussing humanity roundly, but for out of earshot of my young genuine friend.

I made better time than before and didn't even trip on the Lamp Lighter's ladder this time, but saw him setting it up and said, "Hello, nice morning," as I passed.

To which he replied, "You think so, hey." A five mile trek or so to my next planned area of interest, I walked purposely slow as molasses, to think, plan and sight see so as to kill enough kill. Maybe the Women's Exchange will be open after an hour sit wait in Mount Vernon Park beneath the monument.

I saw Mrs. Krumshell open the door and flip the closed sign to open. Before she could pull the window blind up, I was there, standing like a stiff soldier in my stiff starched Live Aid, African continent emblazoned T-shirt, and thoroughly famished with a caffeine withdrawal headache. "Good morning, Mrs. Polly's boss," I said, her name then escaped me. She replied with only a "hmph," but I saw a smile start at the corner of her mouth which she quickly stopped as she saw Polly coming in behind me.

"You're late, Mrs. Kanes," she snapped, but Polly just smiled and said that an automobile was on fire up on North Avenue in front of her house. You could smell the raw, not so unleaded I bet, gasoline fumes coming from Polly's clothes. When Polly had told about the automobile fire, something snapped in Mrs. Krumshell. Her normal frown became a grimace and she snapped, "That's what happens when you have rolling fire balls on the streets. First, they put electricity in the homes and don't even bother to cover and block up the holes where it comes out. Could spill out some night while everyone is sleeping soundly and burn up everything then they put fire burning contractions on wheels" "No sir, I'll use my gas lights, at least I can turn it off at night. As soon as the landlord's men put all that electricity in the house, I stopped up all those holes, to keep it from spilling out everywhere." Well, it was obvious that Mrs. Krumshell would never be labeled a 'Thoroughly a

Modern Millie,' especially as well as that Broadway Show was long yet to come.

Soon, in short order (maybe that is where the term short order cook came along from – never mind) I was again shortening my life span feverishly shoveling in eggs, sausage, ham, toast and the yellow stuff, which I learned are grits and that I really liked. Maybe cholesterol didn't cling so much to the arteries back then/now because people moved about more. Polly dared not sit down with me this time, because of being late I guess, but did holler. Goodbye, sweet nephew James of mine, as I left.

As Polly had just thrown all semblance of early 20th century proper and polite decorum right out the window, I thought I'd give it a try. "And goodbye to you, Aunt Polly, I am off, Tally-Ho and Bully" And blowing her a kiss. As I finished my planned dramatic exit out the door, I heard them, laughing, but also heard the middle-aged man sitting nearby the door start to cough in spasms. Served him right trying to eavesdrop on Polly and my conversation I immediately thought, while he kept twisting this handlebar mustache like the villain on and old silent movie. He probably swallowed part of his mustache. When passing the restaurants outside window, I saw the guy now on the floor with Polly and Mrs. Krumshell tending to him. Geeze, I had to go back, that conscience thing again. Next life, I want to be a free booting sociopath, sans the mill stone of a conscience.

When I got back in the restaurant, a big ethnic looking guy was there now in an apron. He lifted the coughing guy up quite easily, like a rag doll, as he was two heads taller and looked like a machine in shoes. "Hit him on the back,

Spiro!" Polly yelled as man in the apron was already pounding the crap out of the mustachioed man's back, who was now a bright shade of blue, which was good in a way as it made his brown dropping mustache almost bearable to look at.

Instinctively, I pushed Spiro out of the way and grabbed the choking guy around his waist and pushed in tight and quick beneath the rib cage. Nothing, the guy was now limp. Again, I tried, still nothing. Third time, and a ball of half-eaten scrambled eggs flew out past the handlebar mustache and fortuitously into a brass spittoon. Ewww, who would put a spittoon right where people were eating?

The guy started breathing, but again slumped on the floor. Spiro asked me where I had learned to do that. Alarms went off in my head. If I showed him how to do the Heimlich Maneuver, (that I had learned as a life guard and perfected as I had used it two other times, once with my mother and another with a resting hunter on a log I came across on a one of my hikes who was ravenously wolfing down a Big Mac when I interrupted him causing him to start choking) I could really screw up things in that many people who had choked to death between 1909 and its rightful proper introduction would now be saved, and not die. My mind raced, "Where, did I learn what?"

"That thing you just did, you saved his life, son."

"I only did exactly what you did, I just was holding him around the waist, while I pounded his back like you did with my forehead."

Spiro said, "That's not what I saw at all, you were pushing his stomach in."

I replied that I didn't intend do, I was just scared. Spiro asked if I could recreate it, to which I told him I had no idea what he was saying. I just pounded the guy's back with my forehead, whereas, Spiro used his fists. Inside I was in turmoil, this was indeed a crossroads moment. I did exactly what I always do in such sticky situations, I ran. As I ran, I thought, *I guess I'll never see Aunt Polly again or any of them in this life,* I would have to never go near there again. When resting a bit later I stopped to think, did I screw up things already saving that guy, who maybe was supposed to choke to death, there and then. Out of the blue though a calmness and answer to my question came to me. That diner choked because of my histrionics replying back to Polly's over the top goodbye. I caused him to choke, and then I saved him from choking, It was a wash, no harm done, except half eaten scrambled eggs in the full of spit never emptied spittoon and that is not really harm. I was kind of glad to put myself in exile from that restaurant so Spiro wouldn't keep pestering me to teach him the Heimlich Maneuver, as they sold me a bill of goods in that I thought I was getting someone's mom's home cooking and it was really an old Greek guy doing the cooking all along.

Now, straight up Charles Street on foot to find the Johns Hopkins University Campus.

Back, or more precisely, forward in my day, the student body was quite diverse with both sexes and many nationalities represented, but at the risk of being politically incorrect, heavily weighted by the Asian students, who happened to be the best of the world's best. All that were to be seen on my trip by foot today though were young white, collegiate looking type chaps and their old looking by design or the actual old, dark gray/white haired faculty. I grabbed a push broom and a trash barrel on wooden base with wheels attached, so as not to look out of place with my clothes, and started my newly self-acquired custodial duties. One wheel, of course was broke, just like every shopping cart I ever got at home. Taking it all in, while not paying attention to navigating my lopsided non-steerable trash barrel. I smacked hard into three students coming around the corner. Before I could apologize, two of them called me Irish, ignorant trash (my red hair and death parlor, ginger complexion giving me away I guess) and that I'd better watch my place or they'd have me axed. I hope they meant only fired and not really chopped up. Instinctively, I gave them both the finger and said, "Fuck off," but they couldn't interpret 21st century profanity and I guess accepted it as an off-the-boat ignorant Irishman's brogue attempting an American version of, "I'm very, very, sorry to you two esteemed young, learned gentlemen," with my finger being my salute and recognition that they were truly number 1. Joke was on them.

The third guy I mowed into couldn't have been with those a**holes. He was stooping down to help me pick up the spilled nasty garbage from my wobbly trash can on wheels. "I am so sorry, sir, are you hurt, the can's wheels are obviously broken and we, I wasn't as attentive as I should have been." I got up off the floor and said, "I'm fine, Sir, thank you for inquiring." He then replied, " Your very welcome, but I am not a 'sir,' at least not to you my elder." His eyes were that of a young person, clear and soft, with big eye lashes almost feminine. His angular jaw though countered it making sure all knew he was most definitely a young man. Also, unlike the two of a moment ago, this victim of my reckless driving was intelligent and Hopkins material. I introduced myself, and he then did the same, causing me to stagger some. Fate was at play no doubt, here was one of my professional idols of all time, Mr. Abel Wolman himself at nineteen, in the flesh and blood. This man saved, or would go on to save hundreds of thousands if not millions by ending cholera with the innovative design of modern water systems that chlorinated the drinking water preventing the horrible death by cholera. He had the foresight to apply the discipline of engineering to public health care. He knew the full potential of engineering, not just to build or to move things, but to help people stay well, saving and extending their very lives, so as to longer enjoy the things that were built and be carried around by the things that moved them.

Now he asked me if I were well, as I leaned against the wall. I feigned that I had been under the weather, and he asked a few probing medical-like questions then asked who my supervisor was. I thought at last this smart man sees through this middle age liar and he is about to get me fired. Jokes on him. I don't even work here. LOL. as the kids now text.

He said never mind, he would have one of his professor's clear it later, but for now he would take me over to the hospital on the inter campus bus, to get checked out. Believe it or not, it was a real automotive bus. Cloth covered straw seats again, but gasoline powered. You could smell the raw, unburned fully leaded gasoline all the way and some oil in the mix as well, guess carburation science was a little behind internal combustion engine at that point or maybe a two-stroke engine.

Along the almost an hour long ride, which takes now twenty minutes, we really got into the weeds of engineering. Me being very careful not to divulge any of my time's modern-day innovations, or revelations accrued in our Profession in the last since I graduated sixty-five years from now. We both shared ideas, concepts and the theories that we each were loyal to, proponents of, not always the same.

By the time, he helped me out of the bus at the administration building at Johns Hopkins hospital on Broadway (just across from Church Home hospital where Edgar Allen Poe collapsed, dressed as a bum some sort years before, then to die days later in Church Home). I said now I felt much better and ready to return to work, thereby completing the ruse to cover the shock of literally running into my idol who I was heading up to the college hoping to meet that very morning.

Abel replied that was nonsense, that he already got me the day off, paid, and I was going to be examined, just in case. That young man stayed with me all day. The doctor took great notice of my cirra 1960s round inoculation scar, and during the full exam joked that I didn't look Jewish (A reference to my being circumcised, in itself it was not funny but the "you don't look Jewish" was funny. Maybe he went on to do vaudeville and the Catskills.) To their credit, they couldn't find a thing wrong with me as there really wasn't except for my recently diminished case of integrity and truthfulness and no medical test could ever reveal such.

Young Abel was a bit surprised when I treated him to dinner in Fells point just a few blocks south from the hospital. I didn't order any seafood, remembering the smell of the Jones Falls and Harbor from the day before and could smell then and there being in close proximity to the water again, and he didn't have any wine or beer, but unbelievably only water, given that he was orthodox Jewish. After a few beers, the alcohol content in beer was much higher then and boy, you got buzzed fast, I let on that I didn't work for Hopkins as a custodian, but was an engineer employed by the State of Maryland. He said that answered some conflicting observations he had had that day about me. One, that I talked like an educated, professional man not a custodian, and two, that I could afford such a meal. He tried to find out in what capacity I worked in the Maryland Government, but I cut him short and said, "enough shop talk."

It was now dark and Abel excused himself to telephone a neighbor of his mother that he would be staying at the hospital's dorm that night. He had lab work to do there early tomorrow and that would be best. I said I would take a cab home later and we parted ways. Him on to great things, me back for more of that wonderful beer with a punch, a hammer even. After Abel left, and I had more of the unregulated alcohol content hooch – the sky is the limit beer, as always, I started to notice how beautiful the fairer sex really is. This young lady working at the restaurant, was dressed to work hard in the summer inside heat and, therefore, the layers she wore of clothing weren't in multiples of five by necessity as every other woman seemed to be wearing. She reminded me so much of someone I really liked in school, in fact, she was almost identical in every way, her mannerisms, her walk, her swish, her sway…nice. then it occurred to be that this could very well be Cathy's great grandmother. Aww. I shook myself free of the willies I just had and turned away.

I passed out and slept quite peacefully on someone's lawn that night.

People passing by looking at me with pity, a great way to wake up, next to shrub on a lawn beside a sidewalk, that was attached to a gutter. I jumped up and shook myself to show them I was sober and ready again to be an industrious, productive member of their society. Although had I only rolled over only one or two more times to my right, I would have been in both the real and proverbial 'gutter'. God, though my head was hurting.

Like a moth to a candle, I was attracted to the smells of food at the Broadway Market. As my money was running low, I did not feast, but more fasted, on some cheese and bread. I wasn't hungry anyway due to my hangover. By-the-way, wooden wagon wheels and horse's horseshoes on cobblestones can be excruciating loud the next morning after partying.

Then, reeling of booze, real actual grass and I believe my hair head and neck smelled of manure, that pile last night that I rested my head in, evidently, was not the warm soft pillow I thought it was after all.

I was off to find an early turn of the century toy store. Looking for doll house furniture, I soon found out that I could only afford a piece or two. It was expensive, $12 for a tiny dining room set. Thinking it over though, this stuff was all hand made with wood and painted, no plastic, cheap mass-produced imported junk. The clerk saw I was troubled. We talked and I let her know that my gift was to be a special thank you for a little girl's very brave kindness. Upon hearing that, the store clerk then pulled me aside and she said she was aware of an elderly woman that was selling her collection privately and may be willing to negotiate. She asked me to keep quiet about who told me about this. Evidentially, she didn't have a stake in owning the store and was not driven by sales.

Within a half hour I was at this prospect's door, who lived rather close on Anne Street. We had tea, that I think she compassionately added a bit of whisky to, smelling my breath and clothes from the night before and saw me wince at every noise. Only after kibitzing about everything else under the Sun, did we finally get down to business. She let me know that she had long since sold all her doll house furniture and the little figurines. I could have smacked Delores, that was the lady's name, right in the mouth for wasting my time and in those days gotten away with it, except that was not in my nature. My acting lessons from school and limited experience, thereafter, took over. I gently and graciously thanked her for a wonderful conversation and the understanding tea concoction and was about to leave when she said, "all gone, but the damn house," a dust catcher if ever there was one. Well, a fellow swearer. Maybe we could do some business after all?

It wasn't dainty or even pretty, but it was a realistic, three story, Baltimore row house sitting most solitary without the rest of its 'row' though, all by itself. Her brother, long gone now, had built it for her, but she never liked it because she never liked living in a row house. I almost broke down and told her to add a pre-treated timber wood deck on the roof like the urban pioneers were doing throughout Baltimore in my day, and presto, it would then qualify as a Yuppie Townhouse, tripling in price. Delores preferred the big sit alone country farm type house like the one she was raised in outside Gettysburg, Pennsylvania, that, from where she described it was, was very possibly to be one day the farmhouse of President Eisenhower, or the model for it. So fate is a name dropper of sorts.

As the location of the farm was but a few miles from Gettysburg and Delores had to be a teen or in her early twenties there, I just had to ask the inevitable, "What was it like, the battle." After she took a few beats of silence, and started tapping her index finger down on her apron, taking in a breath, she began that as her family and community there and then were Quakers and Mennonites, both armies pretty much left them alone, unmolested, during the preparations and, of course, were too busy to bother her family during the fighting itself. The town and hospital trains from Washington took care of the humans too she found out later, but she did remember the horses and mules still alive, many badly wounded, maimed and dying, from the injuries they suffered from the battle, all seem to find their way to a stream and hollow not too far behind their farmhouse. Even though there were many other streams and shady cool places to rest far closer to the battle field, the innocent animals now all in deep agony that still could walk, many too lame, however' to make it that could be found along the path from the killing fields to their home, all seemed to be congregating or trying so desperately to get to the peaceful spot just behind their house. It was so saddening and pathetic, they all just seem to know to come there, a refuge of peace amid the man-made hell on earth they had just come through, a gate to the beyond just for the pure of heart perhaps that was summoning them in their last moments to rest. "Injured and mangled horses and mules, and a dog here and there, mingling, drinking from our brook, many just laying, staring at nothing in particular, waiting, those that were lucky, quietly passing away as the hours did. Many still with saddles on or trailing fragments of their heavy wooden wagon hitches, still strapped to their badgered and bleeding bodies. They made all kinds of noises in their death throes, human like cries sounding confused and full of a sense of betrayal by those who once cared for them. The innocent souls of man's folly." The men of Delores' family would go out each night and mercifully release those once loyal servants of man from their anguish with guns. Delores remembers each shot sound and the ensuing tears.

Delores said, "My father and brothers were kept far too busy just burying the poor creatures to venture near the thundering rumble and smoke of the battles although they were well aware how bad it was by a constant passage of traffic past the road down by our fence line. All I knew, it was fierce, a hell on earth taking place just up the road. they kept the children in the back of the house away from seeing the sights coming down the road, but couldn't mask the sounds and smells, especially in the quiet of the night." Two months after, my father and a neighbor both had to dig deeper, new wells to get far below the ground water level that was now tainted by the thousands of gallons of battle drawn blood, of both men and beast. We had to all breathe through perfumed drenched handkerchiefs that we carried at all times, both men and women, boys and girls, and sleep under scented cheesecloth draped around the beds until the cold weather set firmly in in about six months due to stench of rotting flesh, such is the glory of war, I still can smell that smell. It's hard to think of the dead in Hallow, respectful, memorial-like terms when each time you remember the blanket of flies that hovered around everything that summer. No patriotic picnic for us who lived through it."

"We didn't discern between north or south invaders, but felt that the evil angel of war, Satan himself, was the only true invader. Changing our hometown into a gigantic cemetery and patriotic bandstand sideshow forever."

Not to rip her off, but all I could really afford was $10.00. After seeing the doll house in her attic, we went downstairs and back out on her front porch for more of that special tea. She preferred that I sit out on the porch so I could tell that my hair still stunk, although I had stuck it down in the lake at Patterson Park. I would need soap to break the oil bond of that manure that came from a quite healthy horse with a varied diet beside just hay and grass. I'd bet a week's pay that he or her had a regular daily diet of green partially rotten apples, along with the flies and worms that reside therein based on the smell of my hair. Thanks to the pervasive stale body odor of everyone though, including dear, sweet Delores my host, now sitting a foot away up wind, the smell off my scalp was almost imperceptible in the communal stew of adverse odors. My post booze headache was all but gone by now. I told her all about Esty, the potential and purpose of this doll house as a heartfelt token of my appreciation to a brave compassionate little girl (hoping to cut a good deal). That her effusive, perpetual, joy, never diminished not even in light of her difficulty in speaking. When I finished my tale, Delores exclaimed with a clap of her hands, "That god damned doll house" as it was a sin for an old lady who never really like it, to let it grow dust, unused, when a little 7-year-old would love it. I resisted, but she said that if I didn't take that God Damn thing out of her house now, that she would take an axe to it for firewood. She reminded me of my great aunt Theresa who would not be born for some five years to come yet, who upon knowing I loved a stereo she had won at a raffle, insisted I take it or she would carry it herself in her wheelchair to her retirement building's incinerator and throw it right it.

With all this said, I offered Delores $10.00 for it and felt more comfortable about it, though such a paltry amount was still offensively low for such a well-made and detailed little brick painted like row, no – town house for dolls. Delores waved her hand dismissively and said no, take it for free or I'll get my ax.

Seeing that there was not much furniture left in her house and her dress was patched in three places, I knew she was in dire straits financially. We struck a compromise. I would take the doll house for free only If she would add a little sign saying, 'Monumental Engineering' and have it delivered to 212 Exeter Street on August 9, Esty's 8th birthday as per her best friend Solomon's information, then I would pay $10.00 for her making the sign and painting on the numbers 212 as well as the delivery. Once I mentioned the birthday, the deal was done. I asked my tipsy host for some paper and wrote a note to be included when the house was delivered:

Dear Miss Esty.

Happy 8th birthday. I am no longer lost and now am back home with my friends and family. Thank you for your kindness and love, your good friend Mr. James Morrison. As I handed it, along with the ten dollars to Delores.

(She never gave her last name) She against all proper, polite, decorum, opened it up and read it. Through moist eyes, she said, "Well I guess you ain't the conning son-of-a-bitch flim-flam man I first thought you were after all." *That's my kind of girl,* I thought, waving goodbye.

As I came in the front door of the Simon's black smith/livery business, I could see that they as a viable enterprise they were on the way out, in the midst being replaced by the automobile. There were dented and fully smashed in fenders, broken struts and springs, any other miscellaneous car parts lying about waiting to be banged out and repaired using the extreme heat and force only available from an old timey black smith. Such being the precursor to modern day precise welding.

The clock in the office showed quarter to eleven in the morning. The blacksmith was a small man, with no bulging muscles that you would expect a blacksmith to have, and he had a discernible Cockney or Liverpoolian accent. I felt good about this as hopefully he was kinder to Solomon then an American blacksmith would be, oh you know what I mean. He wanted 15 dollars to hire out a horse rig and Solomon to help me to move my two very large Steamer trunks from the "Emerald Isle" now berthed in the harbor to my Aunt Polly's house on North Avenue. Of course, none of it was true, I was just enjoying lying all the time now, it had become my advocation as well as my vocation. I only had eleven dollars left. If I did the move myself with the horse and wagon that would be enough, but with Solomon's help all day until dark it was to be fifteen dollars firm. And I had to have Solomon along.

Once again divine intervention. I took my belt off, which was reversible, fine leather with a swivel stainless steel buckle. We talked. I let on that I knew that his business was not as good any longer with the auto becoming more popular. I showed him that if he could diversify, say leather work, boots, shoes, like selling a belt that was brown on one side and black on other. He might even make a go of it, survive the automobile. All the while I talked, he mindlessly was twirling the buckle on my belt, now in his hands that were overly muscular (only that part of his diminutive body that coincided with the blacksmith stereotype) while alternately flipping the belt from side to side, black then brown, brown then black and on and on. Dead silence. Then Simon said, let's split it right down the middle. Seven fifty for my heavy moving wagon with sides and a large horse and Solomon for the rest of the day, that is if you feed Solomon and the horse dinner, wipe down the horse and bring them both back safe and sound, and I'll keep this fancy belt for my own.

Good luck, I thought, I had a 38" waist where his had to be 46" but he wore suspenders. Then it occurred to me that most men then were wearing suspenders. Maybe Simon was planning to innovate and corner the market on belts, reversible belts at that with swivel buckles. Not a dumb blacksmith, another myth blown. "Deal," and we shook hands. "By the way, what kind of metal was used in the buckle?" he asked.

I started to say stainless steel, but quickly recovered. "You should know, I got it when I was in England last year. Your countrymen made it. Boy, was I a first-class liar now."

I handed over the belt and the $7.50, leaving me a grand total of $2.50 in 1909 money.

Solomon had been watching the whole time and had the horse and rig already in the alley.

Before I left, I asked if Solomon knew how to drive the horse and wagon.

"Of course, he can, same as any other man," blurted Simon back. I could tell he was deeply offended by my remark on behalf of young Solomon. As if my comment somehow referenced because of his race, he couldn't manage a horse down the road by himself. I got the drift and did damage control, not wanting this man to think I was just another mindless hick, piling even more vitriol hate upon the boy because he wasn't of the pale persuasion. "No, I mean as a boy, can he legally drive?"

"What are you really trying to say Morrison? Here take your 'belt' thing, find another place." After some self-deprecating insults about my not being able to help the young man if things went awry, if the horse was spooked, pretty much of me being a soft, citified pansy boy, Simon smiled. "Find a man on the street, any of them will help, that's what we do in Baltimore and England too, you are not in Ireland anymore, Morrison."

Simon laughed again, said something about city slickers and said Solomon was more than capable, but he was still a boy, so if those trunks were too heavy, get another man to help, he's not a mule you know. The last part he said most seriously, with no laugh. I understood and my estimation of him just increased sevenfold.

Before we got on the road, or more an alley, I ask Solomon if he thought he could sneak into my basement and get a package I had left there. He replied, he never would 'sneak' anywhere but would go up to Esty's family's apartment and asked her to get it for me. Well, I guess that would work as well, without the adventuresome air of larceny. Ten minutes later the basement doors opened and Esty and Solomon came busting out laughing, with my package in hand. She hugged and kissed me, scaring me some that her parents would see this and then, oh Lord, a fine kettle of fish to be fried. Cliches were never my forte. She wanted to go with Solomon and I, but I told her that the steamer trunks we were haul, heavy, smelly and very dirty. Not for a pretty, little girl to be around. Solomon shook his head afterward and said I lied like a big rug. We laughed.

Solomon had us safely in the stable behind the Belvedere Hotel by two in the afternoon and we, or rather he alone, unhitched the horse from the wagon and put her in a stall with feed for a dollar. She had off the afternoon as well as we. We had about two and a half hours until Mark Samuel Clemens Twain would show up at the Hotel and being a voracious scholar of Mark Twain, having read all his letters, biographies and autobiography as well as all of his works, I already well knew that his train that day from New York would be on time at Penn Station some five blocks away and he would be at the Belvedere at 4:30 sharp with his assistant/secretary. While sitting in the wagon, waiting, I handed the package to Solomon and said, you can't eat it like your wonderful breakfast young friend, but this is for you, for your kindness and courage to care that overrode a normal person's fear to help another complete very strange stranger, young friend. He just stared at me, like maybe I was lying once more. I said, no truly, honest Injun. He ripped the corner and saw it was a book. When finished ripping away the paper, he read aloud the title "The Adventures of Huckleberry Finn." Now silence from him. "For real, for me?" he said through thick emotion.

I replied, "Yes, Sir."

"But all I did was cook you a breakfast, brought you some apples and crackers now and then," Solomon said softly amidst his tears.

"You did far more than that, you unreservedly cared for a stranger, you love our Esty deeply, protect her and help her with her stammering by taking from your precious little free time and read to her hoping she imitates your speech, I've watched you with her from the basement window. I know what you are trying to do. Son, you are more a man than I, and most of the men you will ever encounter, except your father, could ever hope to be."

I wrote a little something inside the cover, I hope you don't mind as it's your new book. He opened cover and started to read it out loud, before I could protest, so I just sat there and blushed.

Dear Solomon, Your father was a very wise man in knowing that your education to be the most important thing you could have in your life, besides love. He was able to give you a great start before God mercifully took him after the unforeseen accident-even by Him, with no suffering or pain in the physical, at least. Use the most important start he and your mother gave you at a great cost to keep ever learning at every turn, don't ever stop learning or caring for others. Remember, President Lincoln learned all he needed only from books, no schoolhouse necessary. With deep admiration, Love, your good friend, Mr. James.

Then only quiet, and the sound not of a young man sobbing, but a little boy letting go, for so many hurts he had absorbed and not registered as that was expected of him from the world he lived in. Then I joined in to make it a chorus. I had never felt this way. Strangely, at that very instant it was no longer me against them, get them before they get me. It just was. And from now on, whatever happens, that is enough.

About 3:30, we went to the entrance of the hotel to wait, Solomon now with 'Huckleberry Finn' tightly held under his arm to be autographed, we hoped. A good reason for us both to be there, a dual purpose for me getting the book that cost $18.00, leather cover with gold inlaid printing on the cover, illustrated. Nothing too good for my friend and the old guy just couldn't ignore this lure, partly by design, but mostly as a gift on par to the quality of the receiver, top of the line purchase, that Sam would then be persuaded to have to stop and autograph for Solomon.

Within ten minutes of standing under the entrance cover, cooler by at least ten degrees than the outside late afternoon June heat, the doorman tried to chase Solomon away. Towering over this guy, with my face now as red as my hair, about to give him an old fashion, ass whoopin', I asked why did he think he had the right to ask my son to move along from a public walkway. Now stammering worse than Esty ever did, he let me know that it was hotel policy that if you had no business there, you had to move along and that the police enforced it. I couldn't let on that we knew his secret that Twain was coming in less than an hour and we were waiting to ambush their famous guest right in front of their hotel. So, I said, "I see, but we do have business, actually a business. My boy is scheduled to relieve that boot jack there at 4 p.m.," pointing to the white shoe shine kid busy at that moment finishing some man's shoes by slapping the rag across them to polish them and remove any stray polish hunks. The door man looked confused and said he would have to check with his manager and went inside. I quickly went over to the white kid now sitting on his stand waiting for the next customer and asked him that if I gave him a dollar and half, all the money I had left in that world, would he let me use his stand to teach my friend how to become a boot jack like I was when I was a boy his age. All I needed was a half an hour to teach him, it now being four o'clock. The boy grabbed the dough, gave me the rags, gave me a quick cursory review of his working inventory and was gone quick as a flash, with the promise to return in a half an hour. I motioned for Solomon who had been curbside, anxiously waiting for Twain, to come here, and put his book safely behind the stand and told him to start polishing my shoes, no questions, quickly. I got up in the chair and he started applying gobs of black polish to my blue Adidas, cloth trainers. (Okay, I hadn't covered every base, so sue me, already.)

I grabbed the Sun Paper the guy left and pretended to read it as Solomon slapped the polish all over my shoes. My feet were now wet inside. He started to whistle and dramatically polish and wave his rags about. A little actor who catches on fast. The doorman reappeared, noticed the change in shoe polishing personnel and customer and was about to say something before I lowered the paper and glared, stone face, piercing him with daggers from my eyes. He turned instantly to watch the street. Solomon finished with me and started on another customer who was waiting and who has real hard, dress shoes. I now squished when I walked. Just as Solomon finished and got a quarter for his labor and a compliment from his first real customer, Mark Twain arrived as did the original white boy boot jack.

There was considerable coughing as the great white sepulcher climbed down from his cab. I could not speak or catch my breath. His secretary ran around and was supporting his one arm while from out of nowhere, Solomon naturally rushed to hold the other, far before the doorman could reach him to assist the celebrity. There was a commotion when the hotel manager tried to shoo Solomon away angrily. He was joined by the doorman tugging at Solomon, thereby tugging at Twain who the boy was holding up. In the warmest southern drawl I have ever heard, Twain said, "Gentlemen, I am not a turkey wishbone for you to gratify your superstitious underpinnings upon."

"Let the boy be, or I will smash both of you with this cane, God dammit it all." They backed off quick and so then I squished walked over next to Solomon, leaving a black trail of wet polish all the way, the whole time glaring at the two Hotel clowns. Inside the lobby, Mr. Twain sat on the first available sofa, coughing and looking so frail. He patted Solomon's knee and said to him, "And where did this young ebony angel of assistance come from pray tell." With this the secretary, the hotel's register desk clerk along with the manager, and the doorman back at his post outside, watched from a distance as Solomon and Samuel Clemens were busy talking up a blue streak. Mr. Clemens's eyes twinkled and were dancing, flashing here and there, alive and youthful, identical to Solomon's, belying the failing body that they were encased in. Two boys happily talking together without a care in the world. As the secretary approached finished with the registration, as he headed back toward his boss. I beelined and cut him off at the pass, as it were, standing next to my friend who was seated next to Twain, hand in hand, and gave him his 'Huckleberry Finn' to be autographed.

The stately white clad old man, then looked my way, my blood now froze as he slowly studied me from head to toe. He seemed to see in me, to see my very soul, my purpose, that I didn't fit in there at that place and time. Mr. Twain, my name is James Allan Morrison and for this evening's excursion, I have been entrusted to be Master Solomon's guardian. "Well, if I never, an Irish red headed, tree tall acrobat, as I live and breathe. Sir, while your middle name reminds me of a long-departed colleague writer of mine from these parts, somehow, I sense that you are a Baltimore Yankee now at King Clemens's court." Did he really sense where and when I was really from? But how?

He asked me and his secretary, and as well as some gawking bystanders who had gathered about, to leave him and Solomon alone for a while "to catch up on real life." We all moved some twenty to thirty feet away, all pretending to be engrossed with copies of the day's newspapers. They laughed much him and Solomon, he lit a cigar, more talking then he opened Solomon's Huckleberry Finn with pen in hand and instead of signing was reading. DAMMIT, I had written my sentiment to young Solomon in the place Twain was to autograph. As he finished reading, he took his glasses off and looked at me, no in me again, and smiled warmly and waved. Then he wrote and stood up, kissing Solomon on the head and summoning his secretary as he started another coughing fit. Solomon scooted over to me with fearful concern in his eyes. I assured him that I knew he would be ok…for now I thought inwardly.

After the fit passed, Twain moved slowly to the elevators by himself. I grabbed his secretary's arm who was rushing toward Mr. Twain. The man shook me off and took great offence at my forwardness. I apologized and said, don't ask me how I know this, if you must know, I believe Mr. Clemens knows, ask him. I went on that his assumption that the cause of the coughing was owing to Twain's insistence to ride outside the Fifth Avenue Stage the day before in New York was completely wrong. The secretary looked at me very oddly. I had only learned that tidbit of information of his thoughts as to the cause of Mr. Clemens current illness, in many years to come from reading the secretary's notes made long after Mark Twain had passed away. Mr. Twain is now having his first major angina attack, an attack to the heart and he needs to rest long and hard starting as soon as possible. He shook loose from me and called me a two-bit soothsayer, charlatan and just another low brow Irish grifter and threatened to call the police if I did not vacate the premises at once. I gathered Solomon and we left just as the elevator doors were closing with Mr. Clemens inside weakly leaning against the elevator wall, once again coughing.

Solomon opened the book once we were outside and let me read what was written by that great author and humanitarian:

My dear Solomon, your older friend is right. I myself didn't have any more schooling than you when my father died when I was young as well. Learning by your hand will stick with you much longer; however, there is a place in this brand-new century for diplomas and such.

Promise me that you and your mother will write me, or visit if you can, in my home at 14 West 10th St. in New York, so we can arrange for you to be tutored to catch up in order that you can attend any college that you set your mind to and gain entry with your grades. In the final analysis though, you may someday curse me for all that civilization, as Huck did the widow Douglas and the whole world.

With great admiration of your parents and deep affection for you, Your new friend, Samuel.

Damn! Lucky kid. Deserved it though.

We got home about eight after Solomon treated me to a bite to eat with the quarter he had honestly earned polishing shoes.

This night I was going to sleep in my new partner Simon's office while Solomon, my surrogate son, slept upstairs in his place. Before leaving though, he gave me a hug that I never wanted to end, but he was almost a grown man. As I drifted off, I could hear Solomon laugh here and there and I knew he was with Huck and Jim floating down that mile wide river under moon light.

Chapter Seven
Tying up the Loose Ends

I woke up and smelled the coffee for real though. I hurried out of the old, tattered sofa I was sleeping in, confused, afraid my coffee maker was left on and would catch my house on fire. Where the hell was I? Then slowly my new reality settled in. The coffee had just been placed there by Solomon who I could hear in the connected barn doing his morning chores. No big weekend breakfast this Thursday, which was fine with me as my stomach felt like I had swallowed hot stones and sounded like a washing machine. Yesterday, the head, self-imposed pain though; today, everything south of the head in turmoil. As I lay on the scraggy sofa, that smelled of everything bad, a wave of early morning anxiety washed over me followed by depression. What if this was it, no going back? I'll have to get a job and make a life here for the next twenty years or so given I was 31 and the life expectancy at the turn of the century was about 50 if I recalled correctly. In those two decades remaining, I would have to walk on eggs to minimalize the possibility that I wouldn't change things so much that the world, as I knew it, went straight to hell. It sounds pompous, but then again there is the "butterfly effect" to consider. It's gentle flutter in the Amazon can snowball and eventually cause a hurricane in the Gulf of Mexico, theoretically any way. I couldn't date, in fear of falling in love and having children, I'd have to be a solitary, working hermit. My head was now swimming as much as my gut was churning. Solomon's strong coffee settled both down.

Both Simon and Solomon entered the shop at the same moment. Simon asked how things went yesterday and I said we moved everything fine to Aunt Polly's house, but I had to use block and tackle to hoist the steamer trunks into her attic. Seems now I had finally evolved into a full-blown compulsive, pathological liar, doing it just as a matter of course and for no other particular reason. The only work I was good for now, if stuck here for good, was that as a politician only and couldn't even consider applying my newly acquired skills alternatively at used car selling, as the automobiles were mostly still all new. Solomon looked down the whole time I spun the yarn. He should never play poker either, like so many I have met in this time. I let Simon know I'd be on my way back to my ship right away and asked that if I may use some paper and a pencil to write a few goodbye notes. Solomon's eyes flashed at me, and he turned and walked in the barn.

It took me about a half hour to write all of my swan song notes, sitting right across from Simon at the desk. We both scribbling away sipping coffee. When I finished and stood up, Simon handed me three envelopes, one for each of the letters I wrote, nothing escaped him, saying, "no charge, on the house." I hollered my thanks for his great service back to the area Solomon had disappeared to, more for Simon's sake than Simon's, and got no response back from the young man. I shook hands with Simon and wished him well, as did he me, and headed off toward Johns Hopkins Hospital, where I had been only a day before.

I could really use their services now as my stomach was flip flopping and the pain was kicking in, but this trip was purely business, and I was flat busted now with no Abel Wolman to get me seen gratis.

As I walked, I wonder where my friends' and family's spirits were now…in heaven waiting to be born or just non-existent, waiting for a spark of life to form them from the universe. Now I was depressed besides sick.

My plan was to slip the letter addressed to the head of the hospital in the letter slot if they had one or under the main door before business hours started at nine. No letter slot and insufficient space under the door so I stuck it in the seam between the jamb and the door. The noise I was making of scratching sounds at the door and my ever-present cursing aroused some interest from within. The door open and there stood the same doorman I saw a day ago while I was in the company of young Mr. Wolman.

The doorman greeted me with, "Why, hello again Mr. Morrison. James is it; how may I help you?"

How did he know my name, I barely noticed him when I was with Abel the other day. I asked, "You know who I am?"

His reply was, "Yes Sir, you are a friend of Mr. Wolman's."

Damn he was the best doorman, I mean security guard, I mean doorman ever. No need for ID's as he kept it all in his head. I was not used to being called 'Sir' by anyone, especially, by someone with such deport and official presence. To this I said, "Sir, you have me at a disadvantage as you remembered my name and I most rudely, didn't get yours the other day."

He laughed a little and said, "No need to, Sir. My name is William, William Thomas." He opened the door wide and there again was that beautiful statue of Jesus. I had zipped past this too a day ago, but couldn't today.

Of all people in need of His help, I was truly lost and in need now. Without a word, Mr. Thomas stood back as I started to pray, like I have never prayed before, at least since before I was seven. I heard William relock the big door and then he disappeared. I missed my family, Ruth, a.k.a Red, my friends, even my pets terribly. My sure, stable comfortable life up to now far away in the twenty first century somewhere, maybe. I was very scared and I fell to my knees crying, asking for His Counsel, His Help. I felt a hand on my shoulder as I prayed which took me back as it must be Him. It was William, Mr. Thomas, who said, "He hears you; it will be fine, have trust in Him." I was a bit embarrassed, wiping my nose as I stood up thanking this gentle, empathic and respectful to all who walked through his door person. He handed me his neatly folded handkerchief.

When I was composed. Mr. Thomas asked me if he could help any more with the business I had there.

Then I remember why I came and reached into my front jeans pocket and pulled out the crumpled envelope asking if he could see that the letter was given directly to the head of the hospital, preferably someone in medicine. He assured me it would be his great pleasure to personally deliver it as they were good friends. You could see he was proud as he made this declaration. He led me to the door and patted my back saying that he was sure my prayer would be answered as he saw it happen so thousands of times.

My letter read as follows:

To the Staff of Johns Hopkins Hospital,

I am not a fool or insane, don't know how, but through Providence's hand I was able to come back briefly from the year 1989. I am not medically trained, but will share the limited knowledge and memory from school about medical progress and facts uncovered up to my time, eighty years from today.

Diabetes: Wasting away, the pancreas over/under producing insulin used to convert sugars to energy.

Cancer: Body's cells out of control, replicating wildly unchecked, chemotherapy using chemicals that only target fast growing cells like skin and hair, but out of control normal cells, drugs that kill fast growing cells will help.

A complete immune system exists within the body that can be taught to 'learn' diseases that threaten the body and need to be destroyed by introducing weakened, attenuated, even killed versions of those diseases into the blood stream, this immune system fails as part of the normal aging process and malnutrition.

Certain molds can dramatically and quickly kill disease causing infections, particularly look at a mold called Penicillium notatum.

The mean life span that you have of 40 will increase to 74 in 100 years so have faith and continue steadfastly in your work.

Mosquitos and ticks carry many blood-borne diseases and spread such in biting into the blood stream thereby directly transmitting those diseases to people and animals.

Mold grown on bread will produce a substance we call antibiotic which can be used to conquer many infections.

Smoking is detrimental to health and causes changes to cells so they grow wildly unchecked as a cancer.

Many diseases are spread by open mouth coughing air borne and through biological, unseen, microscopic, tiny living organisms 'that cling to our bodies using the body's natural oil produced by the skin. Use soap then water to break oil bond attachment of these disease elements, physically washing away these organisms to improve and maintain good health.

Sterilize with heat or alcohol all instruments used to cut into the body to prevent infections. Sterilize immediate outside environment the best you can when exposing the internal body.

Please believe these are true. Test for results as well. My name is, or will be in about a half century yet to come, James Allan Morrison, as I will not be born until 1958. My ancestors did live on Germany Street in your time, changed to Redwood Street during World War I, which will start in Europe in four years. Don't fear losing the war as long as everyone does their part, things will work out and America and her allies will stand and prevail. There will be a great influenza at the end of the great war. I am sorry I have no information on how to fight that as I read that in my time that even though we still have samples of it-the causing virus, a cure for this virus still alluded us.

Again, I am not insane and pray that you have faith that I am a good, forthright, honest man only wanting to help.

If you receive this letter and find it has merit and may further your work in any way and did, in fact, help, then please leave a distinctive marking at the front right (looking from the street) corner of the Johns Hopkins main Administration building in the form of an inscribed "I.D.B.C." and the numbers "12301958" which is, or will be my birthdate. I.D.B.C. is the abbreviation of my employer, The Interstate Division of Baltimore City. I work for the roads department. Also, if room allows also my initials 'JAM.'

Your building still exists in my, time although the hospital will have grown immensely by then helping millions of people and teaching many doctors. Please keep this matter amongst yourselves as the press will tun it into a freakish sideshow circus oddity.

I will check for the requested marking in my time. Thank you all for your tireless work that provided the sound foundation of the advanced medical care we enjoy.

Yours truly, James Allan Morrison

June 10,1909

On my way back to the harbor from the hospital after delivering my note, I stopped by a very special place, nearby and along the way, so the visit did not really exacerbate my already feeling quite lousy and sick.

While all the rest of my friends were looking for cookie cutter ranchers, town homes and condos to live in, John, always the aficionado of the special, the select, chose a very small, old, well-built, old, very small, row home in a solitary small group of about eight or so almost identical copies.

Along what looked like a paved alley, I never did find the "Dallas" Street where John would someday live, however, I did find a small street in the area with houses that fit the bill. There among them was the house that my good friend and road tripping cohort, John, would claim as his bachelor pad in the far future. The whole row of homes was built through the sole effort of Mr. Frederick Douglass, the famous writer and abolitionist that hailed from Baltimore, not originally, but when he broke from his slavery on Maryland's eastern shore and came to Baltimore as a freeman. The atmosphere was odd there. Not of the gravity I thought due to the importance of this accomplishment, but more like a working class set of homes. All the people on the street were white, wherein, I expected a burgeoning African American enclave. First off, none of these people had any idea of who Frederick Douglass was, nor did I judge that they really gave a damn about it once I filled them in. When I explained to the few folks around on this workday of his feats of self-betterment against all odds, they seemed unable or unwilling to grasp the magnitude of this accomplishment of his, the perseverance and fortitude entwined in this man's life. For the people I was talking to at the time, maybe I was out of place and a tad too preachy. They amounted to a couple and their four children in a whirling dervish effort to move their belongings in the house that sat next to the house that would be John's someday. I guess they and their moving crew of two had no time for a primer on American history no matter how close and fresh it was to them and today. The lady, a very large German looking woman, asked what I was about? They had sacrificed a lot to buy this home and was I there trying to undermine it all, by saying it was built by a negro. Now, I only wished the pain that was at that moment churning in my gut, had been since morning, would somehow enable me to involuntarily puke on her in a way that clearly appeared to be involuntary, thereby allowing me to bypass a thumpin' of yours truly by her moving crew, children and husband. They did allow me use of their privy before, I exited, as I was currently needing visits every twenty minutes or so. I could not help thinking they would not have afforded the man who built their new home the same courtesy.

Sadly, I could not be mean to her as she was only a by-product of her times, but also very sadly, this ugly attitude would continue, albeit not so universally accepted nor practiced, up to my time, by more than a few and by choice, nurtured and not of nature.

Walking past the barges, ships and warehouses around the harbor, I was just as wary as I was walking through unsavory neighborhoods of Baltimore back in the future. Unlike the belief of many that things use to be kinder and gentler, that people somehow were automatically better and nicer to each other back then. I clearly recalled the vicious, unforgettable, lifelong unsettling memory of an occurrence that my grandmother told my mother of; that of witnessing a knife murder when traveling the same exact route that I was upon when she was a ten-year-old girl, a few years yet to be, wherein a sailor was stabbed to death and thrown into the harbor for his wallet, by others in similar sailor outfits.

The image of that sailor getting stabbed and killed right in front my grandmother when she was a girl came back as vividly now in my mind as it had a thousand times since I heard that story from my mother as a little boy. Adults really need to censure some things they pass on to their very young.

Now I started seeing everyone around the harbor as sketchy and not the genteel, well-mannered stereotype of people from the 'good ole days.' Coming across Pratt Street it was as busy or even busier at the harbor then, then it would be in my time. Except now people were working hard between the ships and long warehouses and not taking lunch at the inner harbor cafes as they would close to a century later. I was looking for the old U.S.S. Constellation, one of the first ships of the U.S. Navy, that was berthed at Baltimore Harbor, but she wasn't there. Then, "duh" as the kids say, it occurred to me she was at sea, working still, being much younger.

Studying the ships' names, there was one from South America, Spain, and one from Norway, a Side Wheel Steamer from Roanoke and then I almost fell in the water seeing it. There, in front of me, from Great Britain, was the Freighter 'Emerald Isle.'

I was stunned. That was the name I made up in my story to Mr. Berman, the Jeweler, Polly and the Priest Father Christopher, or whatever his name was, as a cover story. I was so proud of my recent discovered ability to lie and fabricate all kinds of imaginative, wild scenarios in rich detail and the proof was right in front of me, it wasn't me at all. I had no idea what was happening, who was really running this show or why. It is not ours to reason why, it seems.

I just sat down on the back of a wagon, between the front of a horse waiting with his wagon behind the one I was on. I started talking to the animal. Whatever the animal, be it a bird, dog, cat, horse, I always chat with them, and they don't ever seem to mind, sometimes they even add or cause critical observations to come to mind that I has seemingly missed in the human world, and its cathartic for me. Well, I just unloaded all my concerns and questions on that poor horse for up to near an hour. When I stopped as the horse now looked bored ,whereas at first, he stared friendly and interestedly at me, more at my colorful T-shirt I believe, there were three guys, crew on the Emerald Isle laughing down at me. As an instinctive reflex, I gave them the finger, that had no effect on them whatsoever, and returned my attention to my four legged friend. Patting him on the head I stood up and started off. Not before all three crew members who had taunted me were standing in front of me. They expressed regret that I seemed offended and asked me to let them treat me to a 'pint or two' to mend things. All three were brothers from the same family in County Cork, Ireland. Patrick, Michael and Daniel Mulligan…go figure, right. I wanted to give in to my natural tendency to automatically go to the negative and warn them about all traveling on the same ship, that horrible thing in World War II when five other Irish brothers, the Sullivans, went down, but could not due to time restraints, not to say there wasn't enough time to tell them about it, but that as it wouldn't happen for thirty-five years, I couldn't. Now I was sad in that I wish there was some way I could warn the grandparents of those Sullivan boys now and save their lives, but even if I could, I couldn't as it could very well turn the future topsy-turvy.

After I realized the crew members weren't going to gang stab me to death since they fed me a nice lunch, and thanks to them, I was feeling no pain at the Tavern they had adopted as their own since in Baltimore, I relaxed and as is my habit, quickly took on their accent and swagger. My talent to mimic as a matter of self-preservation, to get accepted to the tribe. Be it either in Alaska or Africa.

Back at their boat, we all were just sitting on the ground, in the shade of the afternoon summer sun, when a black buggy pulled up and this man got out and started setting up a tripod and then put and old time, I mean modern then, boxy looking camera on top.

It weirdly made me recall that time when I was walking around the inner harbor after work one summer night up in 1986 or thereabouts, when out of the blue a local television crew stopped me and asked me what I thought about the new governor lowering the toll bridges charges.

Of course, I gave them a piece of my mind to show the entire Maryland audience, a negative slant on the governor and the Department of Transportation, only at the end remembering they were my employers. So I quickly added a disclaimer that as I worked for the state, I was sure the raise was needed. Whew.

After the camera apparatus was all set up, I appointed myself the one of our new gangs who would chase this creep away who was disturbing our drunken party in the dirt in front of their ship. However, I am one of those that is more affable when drunk, not mean. The gent's name was Harold and he worked for the city of Baltimore and his job was to photograph each ship that berthed in the harbor to verify their existence, and that the berthing fees and taxes were paid and that the ship had actually been there at the harbor, if later the owners denied it and tried to skip on the bill.

I soon persuaded Harold to include Pat, Mike, Dan and now their new fourth brother, James to be in the photo in front of the 'Emerald Isle.' After a few chugs from the bottle taken from lunch at the Tavern, even Harold got in a photo with us that Dan took. I stupidly asked Harold if we could get a copy, and he said no, they were for official business only, and would be retained in the records. He added that he did not think that between all four of us that we had enough to pay the $38 dollars for a copy. He was right.

A steam whistle sounded that drowned out what I was drunkenly telling Harold to tell his boss to do with those photos. We helped Harold pack up and off he went. We were all getting sober now, and my newfound booze brothers had to get back on ship as the steam whistle alerted them that the final preparations had begun for the 'Emerald Isles' departure. We all said goodbye and lied about getting together in Ireland someday as only drinks can make you plan.

Although shortly after leaving my new crew mates, my stomach was doubling me over now, I had to make it to Key Highway if that's what it was even called back then, almost at the foot of Federal Hill about a mile away on the other side of the harbor. As it was named after Francis Scott Key, the writer of our National Anthem, I didn't know if he had become lionized as a legend yet to warrant naming a major thoroughfare after him. I had read that his grandson was imprisoned in Fort McHenry during the Civil War about a half century before, so they may not have held the Keys in such honor then as we did back in my home time,

When I was a kid, my stepfather and mother were considering buying a three-story end row house that had been her grandfather's. He was a marble cutter and when we visited it, you could still make out the rusty cast iron works where the marble was stored behind the house. Family lure is that he supplied the marble for Ford's Theatre in Washington, D.C., the same marble that John Wilkes Booth, a Baltimore School teacher at one time, broke his leg on falling upon after he assassinated President Lincoln.

When I reached Federal Hill and looked down from it to the property in question, I could see my great grandfather, or some other guy, maybe his assistant, working in my grandfather's back yard. As the man did have a propensity to cuss a lot and had crazy, wild red hair like I do and not many others have such, either then, now, or in the future, I felt strongly that I was his kin.

Careful not to even get close to him, lest something I'd say or do, may cause him to start perpetually fighting with his wife, or maybe just the sight of such a virile, young, epitome of the male specimen as I, might arouse a latent tendency to homosexuality causing him to lose interest in his wife, altogether even. In either case, a conception that would eventually cause me to spring forward could be jeopardize by my simply being there. It's always about me, it seems.

There was no way I was going to walk and I was flat broke. It was really hot, even right up the hill from the water and I was weak as a kitten, so I just sat down on the curb, under the sun, too tired even to find a shade tree along the street. I guess I too was to perish in a gutter in Baltimore the same as Edgar Allan Poe, mumbling incoherently.

It was so hot. Then, like a tiny mirage, a stream of cold water was trickling down hill in the gutter beneath me. I could feel the cold coming off it and the water was crystal clear. Putting my fingers in it I felt it's coldness, I dabbed my face which was burning, hotter to the touch than the rest of my body, simmering in the summer heat. The water was a God send, literally. Where was it coming from in all this heat, in a time of no air conditioning? Once a little revived, I walked hunched over now up to find the spring head of this oasis in the desert. 'Frederick Bros. Ice Company' was on the side of the wagon. It was an ice wagon. I wanted to crawl right inside and just die, the pain was becoming unbearable.

I hunched back down at the rear of the wagon and caught the drips in my hand.

"Brother, I might just have to charge you for that." It was a very skinny man who had an entire black suit on, white shirt and a priest's collar. Here was my angel, of course in black. How he could wear all that in the heat I had no idea? Unless he stayed with the ice all day. "Brother, you don't look very well, maybe go down to Church Home Hospital."

"I just came from there and they said all I needed was rest and to cool down, charged me my last dollar and a half." (The part about just coming from there was the truth anyway.)

"Where do you live, friend? Over on North Exeter Street, the 200 hundred block."

"Sorry, can't help you now, have to make a delivery to 'The Amusea Theatre' down on West Lexington Street. Tell you what though, as the warehouse is over in Highlandtown,

I can pick you up on my way back in a couple of hours, run you home." Now my head was under the drip from the back of the wagon, but with my shoulders leaning against the side of the wagon for support.

Better yet friend, if you don't mind riding in the back and can spare a couple of hours, come along with me on this delivery. I must have that proverbial horseshoe lodged permanently in my lower colon that you always hear about with the Irish. I smiled and he said, "There you go, still some life there." We introduced ourselves, his name was just Brother Richard, no last name given and I didn't ask. The 'brother' part probably had something to do with his white collar. His assistant was his son Richard the second, no last name given either. Maybe it was a habit of working people and tradesmen not to divulge their last names, to keep from being sued.

The ride, while bumpier than my car and without windows, felt just like being in my car in the summer heat with the air conditioner at full blast. I fell asleep. I woke when the doors opened and Richard's son, Richard II, helped me out. I felt a lot better until I tried to stand. It took a few attempts. I was soaking wet from the ice, now I knew I had a fever and felt bad about melting some of my kind benefactor's inventory. I was covered in saw dust that was in the wagon that was used to insulate the ice back then as I recall, it was sticking to my wet clothes. Brother Richard and Richard the 2nd helped me brush it off. These people had to be of the Cloth, God's helpers, of which Church though I didn't much care at this point, just thankful.

'The Amusea' was an old trolley barn converted to show the new moving pictures. As a non-working member of their ice delivery team, I was allowed to go in without paying. Brother Richard said it would do me well, as it was as cool inside as the wagon thanks to the quality ice of Frederick Bros' and the big electric fans blowing over it. I bet Brother Richard's and Richard the second's last name was 'Frederick.' To be fair to me, I was running a high fever and now only a quarter-wit, not my regular half-wit self.

The place inside was packed to the wall, there must have been a hundred people in this cavernous converted to cinema garage, that probably only was meant for fifty. All on the middle of a workday, mostly though they were women and very young pre-school age kids, escaping the heat like I was. I even recognized the women up on the screen…Mary Pickford, they were showing all these really short movies with her dressed in one as a school girl, then an old lady, then a sheep herder, even a boy she monopolized the parts back then. "Jeeze Mary, you job hog, give someone else a shot, why don't you?" And in my feverish state I said this thought of mine on fair play in employment, right out loud, causing more than a few of the young mothers there to clasp their children tightly and move to the other side of the garage theatre. There was no musical accompaniment as the organ looked like it had seen better days with half the pipes missing. So in lieu of sound, they and me after a while, were all reading the writing on the screen out loud in unison. It reminded me of when I saw Rocky Horror Picture Show in college complete with audience participation, toilet paper and water spray bottles, only that now the sing song was without those juvenile attention-grabbing props.

Richard the Second brought me something for my stomach, a new thing advertised to settle stomach aches- Coca Cola and it was cold. I told him I had no money, but he said it was from his dad who said I really helped separating the ice when I laid on it, they didn't have to chop at it so hard, so this and the ride home was my pay. If I didn't feel so lousy I would have been having a blast. In this past week, I had had more than my fair share of unusual experiences, chocked full of varied activities like it was all pre-planned, like those, "If it's Tuesday, it must be Rome," travel packages. *What's the big damn rush,* I thought, if I cannot ever get back. Then I smiled, maybe this, in itself was a clue, an affirmation, that I was only to be there than for a short time. I do believe it was all planned, it just couldn't happen. Now, if I just lived long enough to make it back.

On the way back home, the wagon was now empty of ice, but still cool inside, I again fell asleep. I had never seen the offices of Monumental Engineering in the daylight from the front street. I could make out Esty's father sitting behind the big drafting table through the front window, and I guess his boss, Mr. Monumental just kidding, I never knew his name. He looked professorial though, white, thinning hair, bespectacled, with a paunch. I waved goodbye to my new Richard friends and when they were out of view ran around back to Simon's Shop. I needed to lay down, to use the privy, but couldn't try to sneak back in my basement, in the light of day, with people upstairs, and me all stooped over in pain. I was hoping against hope it was only a case of food poisoning that would soon past, but in the back of my mind I was scared it was worse. There in the alley between my adopted house and Simon's shop stood Lalanya with this very tall blond hair guy, both wearing clothes of such finery that they stood out like a sore thumb. It would have been fine for the Belvedere ball room, not for alley stalking purposes. Lalanya walked right up to me, not even introducing her gentleman friend, not caring obviously if I was a bit jealous or not. Tall, blond, fit, steel blue piercing eyes...why would I be jealous, right?

"James, this is very serious business. You have to start taking it a lot more serious, what you are doing, have done comes with some very far reaching, devastating ramifications," as Lalanya wagged her finger at me my first impulse was to laugh, getting yelled at like a little child by two central casting characters in an alley that smelled of horse and people crap.

"What did I do?" I meant to say it forcefully, in full rebellion, but it came out weak and wobbly as ice water was now in my veins, ever since Lalanya's use of 'devastating ramifications.'

Blondie cupid doll now chided in, "Where is the cell phone battery, Mr. Morrison, we have to retrieve it."

"Probably still with the phone," I snapped back.

"And where might that be?" He snapped back to my snap back. Blondie was plucking my last nerve now, I wanted to say, up a fat rat's ass, but Lalanya was looking at me with real fear in her eyes. "It's okay, it was almost dead when I chucked it."

"Mr. Morrison, we aren't worried that someone will use it to run up your bill, it's the battery, the Lithium in it."

What was this guy, janitor to the world, even talking about?

Now came Lalanya at me, nice cop to blond bad cop.

"James on March 12th of 1954, a little boy playing in that basement where you are now staying will throw that Lithium battery in the furnace, then converted to gas from the coal one now, and the child will die from the ensuing blast." She was crying. I started too as well. Everything went black and white, my muscles all ached. Are you kidding me, how will it come back here, the phone? Hoping they would know that information as well.

Then frosty top joined in. "We don't know. Mr. Morrison, but it will, separate from the phone. We don't know who sent you back here, but they made a terrible mistake. Weren't you trained first as to protocol?"

"Nobody sent me you gigantic Q-tip of a janitor, I didn't volunteer. I am a civil servant, a mediocre civil engineer, not a time traveling clean up man like you." Lalanya just walked up the alley. (Oh, my kingdom for a handful of 21st century Xanax and Imodium) He grabbed my shoulder very hard; I couldn't move. "Mr. Morrison, if you don't fall in line and stop going rogue, you will have to be removed from this time, one way or another. Now once again, who sent you back here, they need to recall you now, at once…you are a liability." Although, T.V. cheesy talk, he was dead serious.

We all went to Berman's: she, he and I. I told him that I was telling my friends here about the quai sun and they were interested in buying it at a good price, say $125 even. My great uncle, the weasel John was behind Mr. Berman and I swear he licked his lips. The deal was made and we walked out of the shop. Not before the little scum bag ancestor of mine ask me to come back real soon to visit.

Blondie, who Lalanya called Christopher, screamed, "The battery isn't here, the old man still has it." He was rushing back, when I yelled for him to stop.

I remember now I took it out before selling it as a precaution. It's safely wedged behind the furnace. Christopher lost it and punched me in the side of the head knocking me in the center of Charles Street where a horse just avoided crushing my head with his hoof. He pulled me up with one extended arm, with no strain at all, this guy was tough. Hid it as a precaution, you imbecile, behind a furnace you placed a lithium battery. Kids are attracted to stuff like that, big furnaces, neat little black rectangular things. That boy sure was…you idiot.

We waited until closing time and all snuck in my basement where, thank God I found the battery. Christopher told me to stay put until he contacted me. They would resolve the matter.

"Look, if you are going to kill me just do it, enough of your bull shit, I didn't ask to come here like you guys. Did you ever think that me being here, doing what I have done is actual part and parcel of the past, an integral part or maybe a necessary correction that was needed, a remedial action?"

"And who planned all this?" said Christopher.

"I don't know, maybe God." This seem to stun Christopher, in his time eventually the concept of someone bigger than his company being in charge was alien to him.

"We don't kill anyone. You are not the first to go astray. If need be, we will take you with us to our time, but that is not a very pleasant option either as you will necessarily be quarantined for the duration."

"I'll save you the trouble, I am very sick, my fight or flight adrenalin charge was now wearing off and the kicks in the intestines were back. Got a feeling it's cholera or maybe just your garden variety dysentery, just give me a gun and a quiet, peaceful, outhouse. No muss, no fuss."

Lalanya was now crying again. Nonsense, Morrison, we will put you on meds tomorrow, it's completely curable, in either case. "What happens if I don't want to…be cured?"

"Don't be silly, James." Lalanya stepped in and I stepped toward her. "Is this Joker for real?"

"James, we all are in uncharted water with this hopping back and forth in time, always will be, reactive instead of proactive, we have to be so careful. No matter how much we try to, undoubtedly changes do occur. Maybe, like you said that is what's supposed to happen, maybe the future and past are a collaborative work in progress, we learning what worked, what didn't, what could cause ultimate destruction, what could avert it, then going back and tweaking things. What you did in leaving a highly volatile lithium substance almost out in the clear to be found and next to a furnace of all, things. My God, James, you caused that little boy's death. In any case, the powers to be, seem to know that the impact of this action, the death of that child would wreak havoc to the extent down the line that now we have to fix it, at all costs."

When she said, "Death of that child," I almost collapsed and now when she said, "all costs" it became crystal clear. It wasn't about me, I was a royal ass to take Christopher's treatment of me personally, he was just trying to clean up my mess and save a tragedy that would occur in forty some years that was done by my hand. He was not saving only the future, but my sanity and my very soul as well. I shook his hand, gave Lalanya a kiss on the forehead, leaving them a promise that I would stay put inside and wait for their direction, that is aside from using Simon's privy, as the inhouse water closets upstairs were not viable. Christopher, while shaking my hand stared in my eyes with his Husky Malamute like piercing eyes for what seemed like an eternity, then releasing his clasp, said, I trust you.

We all three left the basement via the back door, in the broad daylight still, they didn't seem to mind and were in the know about the future, so I assumed, all was okay. Not in the know about every detail as Christopher smashed his man parts on that center pole in doorway as well. As he moaned, I took some pleasure in knowing, he was as fallible and human as I. Now the commotion was over, the turmoil in my gut was back and pressing me off to Simon's dual sitting privy.

I was really feeling lousy at this point. I just made it back to home, when I went into Simon's office and asked if I could sack out in the barn for a little and use his privy as my ship was delayed one more day, and I thought I might have eaten some bad food. I promised Simon this would not be a habit of mine and I only needed a few hours. Both he and Solomon helped me to the privy about six times that day, between my collapsing back on the mattress of Solomon's they had dragged down from upstairs.

When I awoke the last time, it was dark. Simon was gone for the day, but there was Solomon in a chair sitting over me reading the rest of Huck Finn.

"Are you hungry?" he asked.

"No, but I am sure thirsty." The pain in the stomach was still there, but I was empty all around and now shivering with chills. We sat like that for an hour or so, me dozing while he read.

Finally, I got up and said it had passed, whatever "it" was and I was going home to my basement across the alley. He knew I was lying once again but said nothing. I hugged the boy then shook the hand of the young man that stood before me, wise beyond his years, with a heart and smile as big as the world, and then said, "Bye for now," full well knowing this would be the last time I ever saw him in this life, the last fib I would ever tell him. He said nothing. I told him to wash that hand I shook of his with soap right away. Made him promise. Getting back into the basement I saw that Esty had left her best doll laying on top the crates with a cloth on top for a blanket. On the plank underneath, she scrawled, "So you won't be too lonely all by yourself. I left you my new doll, Becky Thatcher to talk to!" Wow, what a kid.

Now back at home, empty, and feeling all wrung out, all my worries, concerns and fears vanished. I wouldn't die alone in that basement only to be found by those two sweet children, who only knew I was there, thereby scarring them for life. Just what Solomon needed, seeing two dead bodies by his mid-teens, I wouldn't, couldn't screw up things any worse as Lalanya and Christopher were now on the case. And maybe my fight with the world, with every perceived slight or threat, my hot, cold reaction to everything would be tempered somewhat from here on in. I was a fallible human after all. Not qualified any longer to issue judgement on anyone. Not qualified to hold a grudge or not forgive for the rest of my days, The idea of causing a death, particularly of a child is quite humbling. My time here was about up anyway. Tomorrow they would come for me and who knows, let me give living in-the-near future past my time a try for a change of pace.

I fell deep in peaceful sleep, first time in a week, only to be awaken by the most severe pain I ever felt, maybe I had an appendicitis, it was centered on the right side. About an hour later all the pain just went away. Now I was worried as that is usually what happens when the appendix ups and bursts inside you. Enough already.

I had been pushing this reoccurring nagging thought out of my mind since I got here using the thought stopping coping strategy, I had learned in a comprehensive three credit course I took in College for Stress Management (the most life changing and valuable one I ever took). The first-time little Miss Esty saw me, or partially saw me, she said I was transparent, she could see through me like her mom as a girl did with her brother Randy who was now sitting on the foot of her bed, but who had just drowned in a lake. Maybe, this was all a post life dream, my soul still clinging to life so much so to manufacture and fabricate an entire elaborate rich textured world of my own imaginings. Or perhaps this is all real and I just as real, but instead of being produced cell by cell and then born, the necessary cells were drawn together and solidified to make me now, a complete human, clothed, in only a few moments thereby explaining my transparent to solid state that Esty saw. That child is either the bravest and fearless or has the faith of Job, not to have screamed and ran away witnessing such, as I would have, running fast as the wind and crying like a little school girl not of Esty's bravery all the way.

My head was swimming. Now, back to my 'thought stopping exercise,' there a lot better.

Always being the one who has the last word, knowing I would probably not be here as of tomorrow night, either taken by Lalanya and Christopher (that 6'8" living, breathing, strong as hell, walking Q-tip swab associate of hers, I bet he can dance for real unlike me, bet he takes her the Belvedere all the time) or from peritonitis, from a rupture appendix, I better write some letters before I go.

First one to Esty's parents, second one to Solomon's mother and the third to the Baltimore Sun Paper, then I better get to sleep to start my new life tomorrow looking for a job and a place to live or getting vaporized to go, not so quietly, into the future.

I thanked Esty's parents for her and her child like faith and wonder. I asked them to believe her and Solomon as to my existence and temporary stay. To even talk to Mr. Percival Taybeck of Roland Park for verification.

To Joseph, Esty's father, and new junior partner at Monumental Engineers. I briefly let him know that steel would be the future in all construction, wholly replacing cast iron and gave him a primer on steel reinforced concrete. To prove that neither his daughter or her friend constructed my letter to him, I left a particular difficult and complex calculus problem for him to solve and told him of where I had hidden the answer in the basement to check his work when completed.

Furthermore, I left him with a personal anecdote from my family regarding Esty's recent onset of stuttering about the same time they tried to break her of being left-handed. My grandfather was born or about to be born in four years, left-handed as well. And he too would be chastised and berated to change from his natural preference to using his left hand, because as with Esty everyone unbelievably believed that somehow left handedness was a mark of badness, even evil. Very soon my grandfather, began to stutter and did for some 30 years until married with a family. I shared that science in my time proved that left handedness was simply a matter of genetics, what cells (genes and trying to talk to him on that subject would be altogether alien to him as their discovery was yet to be as far as I knew) we got from our parents and was not bad or evil or wrong in anyway, but just was. And lastly, I shared with him that we had learned in my time that such efforts to force use of the right hand in conflict with the natural urge to use the left creates many physiological problems, with a major one being the onset of stuttering. As a man of science, I hoped this would be enough. Closing with "have a happy life, your friend and colleague, James Allan Morrison, P.E."

To Emma, Solomon's mother, I asked her to believe Solomon and Esty about me. That I was no ghost or demon, only an unwitting passenger through an odd burp in time. That I was a God-fearing man of flesh and blood that will live out his life 130 years in the future, but promised to catch up with her, her husband and Solomon in heaven some fine day in both our futures to prove it. Lastly, I told her about a Mr. Enoch Pratt, who would donate and build Baltimore's first free public library system very soon and that given his fine intellect and love of books, that Solomon should contact him directly to be involved from the ground floor up.

I debated whether to let someone know of the impending Titanic tragedy in only a few years from then and even the third assassination a U.S. president in a half century. I decided not to.

In my letter to the Baltimore Sun, however, every time I began writing, my words vanished as soon as I had written them, so that matter was settled by whomever allowed this trip. Maybe it was not a glitch in time after all. Maybe the things I was supposed to address weren't earth shattering, not yet anyway, but smaller in scale, that wouldn't change things overall in a fluttering butterfly wing cascading effect. I felt that I was not in control or had to be and that was most comforting and reassuring. The crushing anxiety that I was operating under for the last few days lifted all at once, and now I was ready to go home. I would sorely miss Esty and Solomon and all the others I met here, but I missed my world too.

With it all done, I placed the letters on top of the crates, took my remaining "As-Built" Plan Sheets containing only the information added after June,1909 and folded it down so to fit in my back pocket and secured them there. I was ready to move on and out, first thing tomorrow, "damn the torpedoes."

While reclining back against my stacked wooden bolster pillow, I accidentally kicked over the bottle containing the Great Baltimore fire debris that made the trip along with me and the as built plans and that I had all but forgotten about-out of sight, out of mind, breaking this one as well as I did the other and causing another mess identical to the one in my office a few days ago or more precisely eight decades to come. I got back up and started scooping the oily mess up when I felt myself going down with all color disappearing, first to gray, then black.

I woke up Monday morning with everyone in my little office as paramedics prepared to take me to nearby Mercy Hospital. Of course, the rumors ran wild that I had holed myself up in my office over the weekend on a binger, but tongues will always wag. Those close to me, both at home and in the office, knew this could not be true anymore thanks to the early onset of chronic acid reflux the only thing I could drink now was milk.

The hospital, (by the way, the same one that I had my tonsils taken out in when I was five and the same one where they wheeled my first boss, John the marine and amateur dentist, you remember him, to during his first heart attack while still sitting in his office chair as the hospital was that close to the office. That heart attack was caused partly, if not entirely by me always being at odds with him over everything as that was my nature, then. Cut any perceived threats off at the pass then crush, kill and destroy in my personal scorched earth policy-even with those I love, sometimes even more so with them. Later I would apologize to John, and we became best of friends for the rest of his life) cut me loose two days after fluids for dehydration and zinc supplements. Turned out that pesky diarrhea and stomach cramps was not food poisoning or even an appendicitis, but cholera as I originally thought, as I was very susceptible not possessing the 1909 accrued tolerance, if there even was one. Nice to know that Abel Wolman long ago took care of that problem for us today in his time then.

Hazmat took the open and the remaining bottles of the Great Baltimore fire slop that I still had in my office with them and in a later in a report, stated that the gases from that sludge are most likely what caused me to pass out and the ambient fumes in the small office with no A.C. or ventilation over the weekend, kept me in a coma like state until the air conditioning circulation systems were turned back on early Monday morning.

They had called Ruth, a.k.a Red, and she came back from her vacation at the Ocean that I had declined to go on with her because, ostensibly, 'I just had too much work to get done.' She came back alone, early, not alerting my mom so as not to unnecessarily, alarm her, especially if she found out that I was just on a bender locked up in my office, again, as in the old days. When she got to the hospital about noon there was a big hoopla as they were not going to let her in. At first, I chalked it up that they had me in that negative air pressure quarantine room and so I started yelling for them to let her wear one of the protective suits the nurse and doctors were all wearing. Finally, though, I discovered that was not the reason. They said as she was not family, wasn't my wife, they could not let her in as I had a no visitor restriction for persons outside my immediate family.

Jesus Christ, we were almost Common Law. eight years together must count for something. "Let her in!" And just then, maybe the IV contents, maybe my guilt, maybe the expansive mind-blowing experience I had just went through, if in fact, I had not imagined the whole thing, what I had just yelled out the door kept ringing in my head, louder and louder, amplifying how stupid, how selfish I had been. Why Red let me do it, I don't know, but I had strung her along now for eight years, most conveniently using my responsibility of caring for my mom as a reason. I knew that Red loved her as much as she did me, differently of course, and still threw my mother's care and wellbeing up in her face every time the subject reared its head as an insurmountable wall to marriage, to progressing on, to her and I having a full life. How could Red balk at my wanting to care for someone that we both dearly loved, check mate. Always in battle. What a fucking idiot I have been. It was unforgivable and I now clearly saw it in one great flash, an avalanche of guilt.

All was deathly quiet for about a half of an hour, and I imagined that Red just up and left. That was okay though, as I would later cover it as not being my doing, but the hospital's stupid, unyielding regulations, my 'Get-Out-Of Jail' card (old habits die hard). However, in planning this, yet another evasive maneuver, one of thousands I had launched over the years with her, I stopped and gasped, felt that this was one of those pivotal come to Jesus moments in life where the game had to stop then and there. That this was the one last chance she would give me ever. *Do something now, this instant or lose everything forever.*

I thought of all the dear friends I had just made, talked to and loved and realized that I begin to learn to care deeply and genuinely about people I left behind back then, if in fact I ever was, and how in an instant they are all gone to me forever. The stream of it all keeps flowing and if we don't hold on so tightly to what we have, we will be separated for sure from those who were given to us to float along with us all the while, making it all bearable and the journey, with its bumps and blind turns, rapids and falls, all worth it and fun even.

Before I could muster the courage to remove the IV's and run out of the quarantine room with only my gown on, that never-tie-in-the-back one, chasing after Red like in one of those windy swept haired women on the cover of ever Harlequin Romance pulp novel ever cranked out, the nurse made it back in the room.

"Becky the nurse" as she said was her name and even had it engraved that way on her white enamel ID pin, and how she signed the white board listing all my personnel's names assigned to care for you that was hung at the end of my bed up on the wall, (who had three boys, two dogs and a man child for a husband, as I learned because she generously shared about her most precious things in this world with me, even though I shared nothing with her, the same 'Nurse Becky' that although protected by a mask gloves and face shield, regularly, no, all the time, came in to my quarantine room again and again, something I wouldn't' have ever done, at least not a week ago, maybe now), came back into my room Unlike her normal all business-like quick step, with a dancing side foot slide here and there, she now walked slowly and haltingly. This must be bad news. A turn for the worse. She was standing sidewards so all I could see was her telltale Baltimore Orioles sticker that her youngest had slapped on the corner of her face shield.

Then I could see Red's telltale long black long hair cascading down and standing out gloriously down the back of the nurse's top.

She was a winner, no doubt. The real thing, in any and all time, I did not deserve her and she sure as Hell didn't deserve how I sometimes coldly, took her deep unwavering love for me for granted.

In my newfound propensity to tell untruths, one more little white lie. I told Red that I had gotten a sub from one of the dives on Baltimore Street next to our building and heated it up in our office microwave, which over the years it had been in use had a good accumulation of many crusty stalactites hanging from the bottom of the top side of the microwave, comprised of portions of thousands of meals gone by, allowed to boil over and pop, and I was sure that is what happened. Food poisoning. Red replied, "It doesn't matter now really, Jam, but they said it is cholera, not food poisoning. You were down in that filthy Jones Falls by that God damn bridge, weren't you? Did you get the goods on your latest sworn enemy? Was it all worth it? The fight won?"

Nothing was said by either of us for a time, we just watched the T.V. overhead mindlessly.

"Did you leave Mom in the car, or drop her off at the house, before you came?"

What are you talking about, she doesn't even know, I came up directly from Ocean City, left your nephews with Mrs. Clarence in the upstairs condo. She didn't even go with us, she's too busy working.

Working? Where? What…down Ocean City? Did she get a job over the weekend, like seasonal?

"What's wrong with you. She makes enough after her thirty years with State Highway not to have to work a second job anymore, you of all people should know that. Are you OK?"

My head was spinning, my blood ran ice cold once again and not from anything in the IV's.

Although, if I had enough time to retire and at her position level, I'd be out like a flash, bee-lining all the way to my condo "downy ocean" as the locals say.' I was in screaming turmoil inside, but calm outside, "How's she feeling?"

"About what? What do you mean? She's healthier than both of us put together. Says she wants to work until maybe she has forty five years if she can make director of human resources in the next five years. She thinks her boss, Carolyn, I think that's her name, will be going next year maybe."

It worked, unless I'm dreaming this whole thing, or dreamt that Mom was an invalid thanks to that Taybeck shit, it worked.

"Hey, did she ever tell you about that old boss of hers? Taybeck, I think his name was… a real creep?"

"Who? Never heard her mention that name."

It worked! Maybe I didn't change anything back then that wasn't meant to be, a remedial correction all along. Maybe people go back all the time and fix things. Could be going back doesn't destroy the world or lives that exist today but corrects a course that could have destroyed it and people, or changed them irreparably, if let be. Going back might be like finally finding the right jigsaw puzzle piece that had fallen on the floor under the table and picking it up and taking the one you forced in its place away and finally putting the right one in, a perfect fit.

Guess it's the drugs talking. "Hey, Ruth?" At this she swung her head around from staring at the TV hung up near the ceiling. I hadn't called her Ruth for, she just couldn't remember how long. "Eight years is one tenth of a person's average lifespan now in America, one tenth i.e. 10%. I guess we've test ridden it enough. Yuk, I didn't mean to say that. I mean to say, I think it works fine except all the distance in between. What do you say, we just get to it."

"Jam, James, what are they putting in those bags?" she pointed to the IV pole.

"Viagra in the right bag and sodium pentothal in the left, I think. I will, if you will?"

"I guess that's the best proposal I'm going to get, huh?"

"Good things come to those who wait, but seriously, I can and will do better, you'll see, promise. Besides, right now you look like a frigging spaceman, hard to cozy up to that."

"OK. JAM, Jim, now shut up and let me finish watching this tv show in peace." She slipped her hand into mine and squeezed.

The first day back at work I left the office at lunch and hiked the long hill from my office the six or seven blocks to Johns Hopkins Hospital. I took my hard hat so I wouldn't arouse suspicion searching around the base of the old Hopkins building. I took off my orange hard hat and had it under my arm as I entered the door, immediately there stood the statue of Jesus that I now believed I had prayed under away back when.

Made me think about the modern medical information that maybe I really left here some eighty years ago as a crib sheet of sorts, Did He approve? Was it by his design or was the whole business a freak of nature outside of His control and maybe the design of others, Hell bent on undoing his plan by creating more overpopulation with the people that that information saved and their children and their children and its accompanying misery and grief.

I half looked for someone in authority who would give me the green light to perform a cursory review of the building's brickwork around the right-hand front corner of the old original entrance to the hospital, and half didn't want to find anyone so as not to bother to have to explain in order to get permission. I found none, only the guard who was quite friendly. Turns out his brother was a guard at my building that sat across from the penitentiary, James being his name as well.

James was the one who gave me the great advice to stop dancing and tormenting the prisoners in response to their cat calling to me through their grated windows. James told me that my teasing them with replies of "I am out here and you're in there." All the while doing that little dance of yours next to your car was parked next to and just beneath the Maryland Penitentiary open cell windows was not the best idea as most all of those bad boys will get out eventually. "Oops"!

The guard's name, James' brother, at Johns Hopkins was Henry, and after a bit of small talk and out right falsehoods on my part, he gave me the okay to search to my heart's content, as long as I restored any disturbed grass or soil. While writing down my cell number for him to give to James to have him call me to catch up on old times, I noticed a familiar face behind him on the wall. Amongst the stately professorial and stern looking old white men doctor types, there he was, William Thomas, smiling down. Maybe, it all did really happen.

Holding my breath and crossing my fingers, I walked around the front of the building. The sun was glinting off of something in the corner where I was heading. It was a brass wall plate of some kind. For a moment, I thought that instead of etching on the brick, as I had asked, that maybe the then director of the hospital put my requested code of acknowledgement on brass. No, it was a brass standpipe for fire hoses to connect to. An area of about three-square feet of the brick work had been replaced by this connection plate right in the area I asked them to etch in my coded notice. Wouldn't you know it, I was crestfallen.

But in looking closer I could see the faded remnants of professional engraving in the brickwork just to the right of the brass standpipe plate, I could clearly make out the letters 'B.D.C.' And on the next brick to the right '12301958 Cheers! JAM,' my birthday and initials. All very small and engraved. It all did happen for real, I sat on the grass and cried then laughed.

Later in laundering my very smelly and stained clothes wore during the weekend shut up in my office, Red found the embroidered handkerchief that Hopkins' doorman William Thomas had given me, with the initials WDT. At first, I kidded her that it stood for Wild Dame Tonight, but then I sat her down and told her the entire story. We just named our second child, our first son, William Thomas Morrison

Later, much later, I reluctantly gave in and researched what became of both Esty and Solomon, I learned that Esty became a speech pathologist at Johns Hopkins of all things and of all places, with three children and 11 grandchildren and passed away in her sleep with her husband and family by her side at 82. Solomon had a career and achieved the position of Deputy Director-Chief Librarian for Enoch Pratt Library for 43 years, authored four books, one a tribute to Dr. Martin Luther King, and died instantly from a brain aneurysm on his bus ride home one day, a month after his 100-year-old mother, Emma, had passed. He was reading a book, then suddenly and peacefully slumped against the bus window with the book dropping slowly to the floor as his grip and life subsided away. He was 84 and never married.

Another revelation was that my father gave me a sizeable bequest that had been handed down from his great grandfather, Charles Allan Morrison, to be given only upon my marriage and/or the birth of my first child (we in our family were always laid back as to the rules of matrimony relative to having kids, even way back then) and at that time shared equally with my brothers and sister. The portfolio dad left me and Ruth, and that was given to us by Mom at the end of our wedding reception was filled with old U.S. World War I war bonds and newer Savings bonds, that when totaled amounted to $2,870,000 at maturity which long ago passed. Inside the old thick expanding leather binder that was once emblazoned sharply with the company name of 'Taybeck & Sons, Consultant Engineers—Baltimore—New York—London—Amsterdam, now faded with the leather full of small cracks, were also two letters, both handwritten. they read as follows:

Sept 23 1948
Hartford, Conn.

Dear Mr. (Jam) Morrison

In balancing out all my Ledgers, of all kinds and makings on this earth, today upon my one hundredth birthday, I would be remiss if I did not settle accounts with you as agreed upon.

Pursuant to our informal contract for your invaluable expertise provided on that summer afternoon in 1909, during our working lunch and dinner toward the betterment of the Taybeck Set on Grade Cofferdam System, you will find enclosed an amount of $2,850,000. in U.S. issued bonds, of which the last of will reach maturity by the end of this year 1958. Also included, a draft check to cover the difference to-date of your share of the overall gross at the agreed upon percentage of all royalties received for using our patent to date, I dutifully and diligently endeavored to again locate you a number of times, subsequent to our meeting, in order to fulfill our agreement, with payments on an annual basis, but to no avail.

I believe myself to be a man of science, that is my stock and trade after all. Maybe not the best of engineers as you showed me, but a man of integrity who keeps his promises. How you came back to my time and how you returned to your time, is, to say the least, beyond my comprehension. Only the Good Lord knows or should know I take it... My search over the years, did turn up a man with your name, who lived in Pittsburgh, Pennsylvania, who worked as a laborer in one of Carnegie's original hell hole steel plants that was subsequently bought up by J.P. Morgan's U.S.

Steel and made worse. Hope you didn't have to live through those bastards sorry that your kin had to. As you now know that was your paternal great grandfather, James.

Know that he was a good, upright man. Looked like you only with straight red hair. I hired him right off and he and your great grandmother as well as your grand aunts, Emily and Alice (your grandfather was yet to be born), relocated to our Baltimore, Maryland office.

The cofferdam system of ours, your name by the way was appended to the patent) was last used just after the Second War in occupied Japan. The sum included herein is the 2.5 % as agreed upon with interest compounded.

I and my family will be forever indebted to the invaluable contribution you made to our design.

Hope someday to again meet you in a place where cofferdams and the like, all things physical, are not needed anymore.

With Great Admiration,
Respectfully yours,
Percival Taybeck, Chief Engineer (Emeritus)
Taybeck & Sons – consultant engineers.
(As dictated and faithfully recorded by James Morrison, II)

P.S. Included is your Maryland driver's license, effective December 13, 1981, that I lifted from your billfold when you evidently dropped it by my water closet commode after our working lunch break. The other letter inside the binder was both from my mother and father:

Dear Jimmy,

We were as astonished as you must be at this very moment reading this. Maybe not though as you were the one who went back there and then.

Our heads still hurt trying to comprehend all of this. We have never kept secrets from you and your brothers and sister, but for this one, that we inherited from you… Now on your wedding day it is yours to keep and share with your siblings and your soon to come children and grandchildren, God willing.

The amount in the binder has been reduced a bit over the years to cover the cost of yours and your sister's and brothers' educations as well as our condo in Ocean City and the hospitalization and recovery medical costs from that horrid accident when you were hit by that car in the country when you were ten.

Not now, but after your impending honeymoon that starts this very night, when you are back and settled, we can sit and go over this all with you and your wife.

Love Dad and Mom.

Finally, even given my research that the contractor could have easily known the nature of soil regarding load bearing ability, I was still overridden, and my boss took off so he wouldn't have to approve payment of the bogus claim, but others did. The governor's buddy got his million and, therefore, the grand old hotel is no more. A mere shadow of its once stateliness and grandeur, now a collection of cookie cutter condos. Cest la vie, it was a nice trip anyway.

A month or two after I was back, feeling great, immersed in the 21st century again I started to wonder if the As Built Plans for the Penn Station were back in the Archives again, as I left them back there and then. I kind of was curious if there might be any of that old slime around in jars too…possibly for a return trip.

I wore my jeans and old live aid T-shirt as I had before, tracking through the archives. I found the old wooden box which was odd as I never took it with me back there or returned it from my office now in time. The plans were all there, finalized and signed. My notes to the engineer back then had all disappeared though. More importantly, there were no other bottles of oily great Baltimore fire ash to be found. My ticket to ride was gone, the window closed for good.

While I was in the archives, I had one more stop to make. After spending the entire morning looking with a very knowledgeable and anal retentive clerk, I located the harbor tax files for the end half of 1909 June through December. There was the file marked UK Shipping and a thin brown folder among eighty or so, labeled 'The Emerald Isle.' I took a breath and reached inside. In the center of the tri-folded bunch of now yellowed documents were three photos, one just of the ship, one marked "Mr. Harold Wolf, Baltimore City official photographer June,1909," and one just marked my friends, Patrick, Michael, Daniel and James – crew members of the 'Emerald Isle.' In that picture, there I was one with them, in living black and white.

I was there. I borrowed the pictures and copied them, blowing them up. They now are on my office wall and when asked about them, as I always am, I just say they were some really old friends of mine that I met on a trip you wouldn't believe.

Ingram Content Group UK Ltd.
Milton Keynes UK
UKHW022058230523
422235UK00004B/27